I0714593

2

Portals:

Book One

Beliefs & Black Magics

Travis I. Sivart

Portals: Book 1, Beliefs & Black Magics

Copyright © 2020 Travis I. Sivart

All rights reserved.

Cover Art by Stefan Keller

Cover Design by Travis I. Sivart

ISBN: 9798668332816

Talk of the Tavern Publishing Group

Dedication

To those that seek different places and different worlds.

8

Table of Contents

Dedication 7

Acknowledgements 13

Chapter 1 20

Chapter 2 28

Chapter 3 36

Chapter 4 46

Chapter 5 56

Chapter 6 66

Chapter 7 76

Chapter 8 84

Chapter 9 92

Chapter 10 100

Chapter 11 108

Chapter 12 116

Chapter 13 124

Chapter 14 132

Chapter 15 140

Chapter 16 148

Chapter 17 158

Chapter 18 168

Chapter 19 176

Chapter 20 186

Chapter 21 194

Chapter 22 203

Chapter 23 210

Chapter 24 220

Chapter 25 228

Chapter 26 238

Chapter 27 247

Chapter 28 256

Chapter 29 269

Epilogue 273

Sneak Peek of Portals, Book 2, Demons &

Daggers 281

Calendar.. 289

Glossary 291

Special Thanks 301

About the Author.. 303

12

Acknowledgements

I'd like to recognize Eric Ugland, author of 'The Good Guys' series and much more, who inspired me to bring together stories that I wrote in my teens and in 2013 and combine them into a brand-new thing that is this book. I loved writing it, and give a fair amount of credit to Eric. Thank you for your books and the chats.

14

Travis I. Sivart

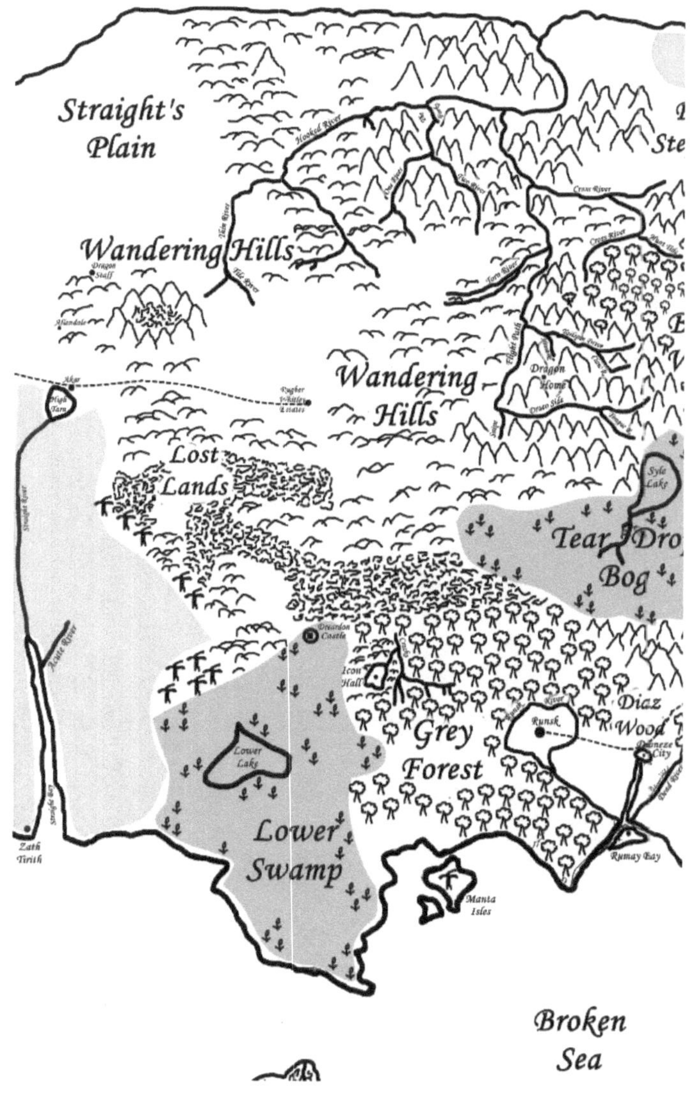

Straight's Plain
Wandering Hills
Wandering Hills
Lost Lands
Tear Dro Bog
Syla Lake
Dragon Staff
Islandale
Akar
High Tarn
Rugher Ratley Estates
Dragon Home
Dreardon Castle
Icon Hall
Grey Forest
Diaz Wood
Runsk
Deineze City
Lower Lake
Lower Swamp
Zath Tirith
Manta Isles
Rjemay Bay
Broken Sea
Straight River
Acute River
Hooked River
Tile River
Torn River
Cross River
Flight Path

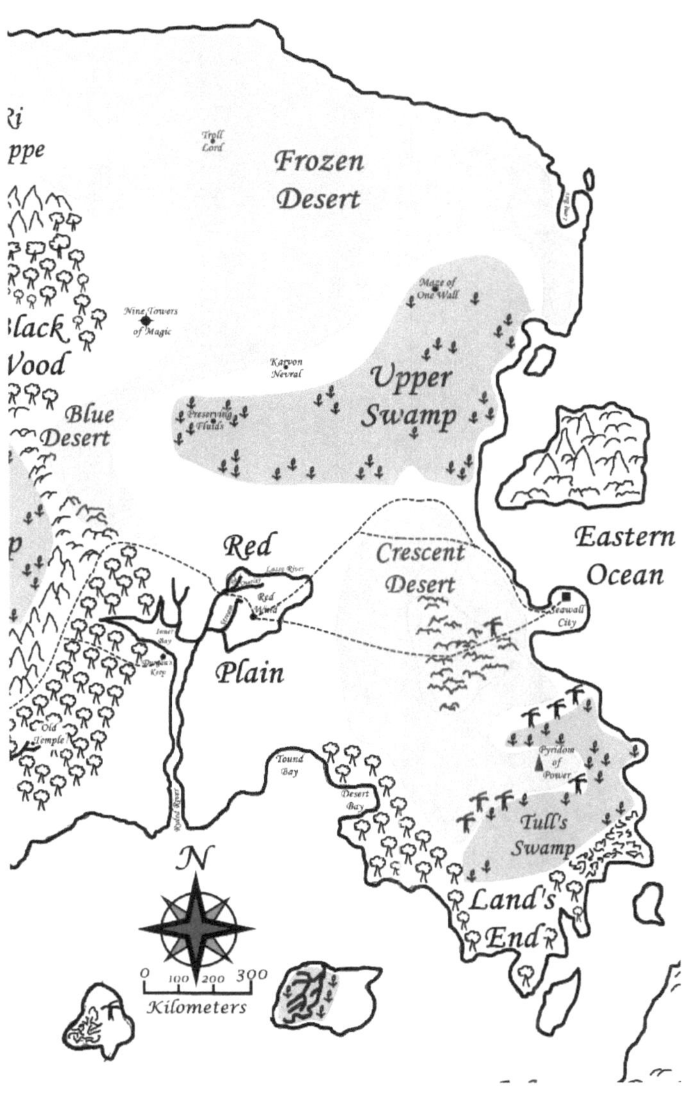

Frozen Desert
Troll Lord
Long River
Maze of One Wall
Upper Swamp
Nine Towers of Magic
Black Wood
Karyon Nevral
Blue Desert
Preserving Fluids
Eastern Ocean
Red Plain
Loser River
Red World
Crescent Desert
Seawall City
Inner Bay
Limpid
Dragon Keep
Pyridom of Power
Old Temple
Tound Bay
Desert Bay
Rebel River
Tull's Swamp
N
Land's End
0 100 200 300
Kilometers

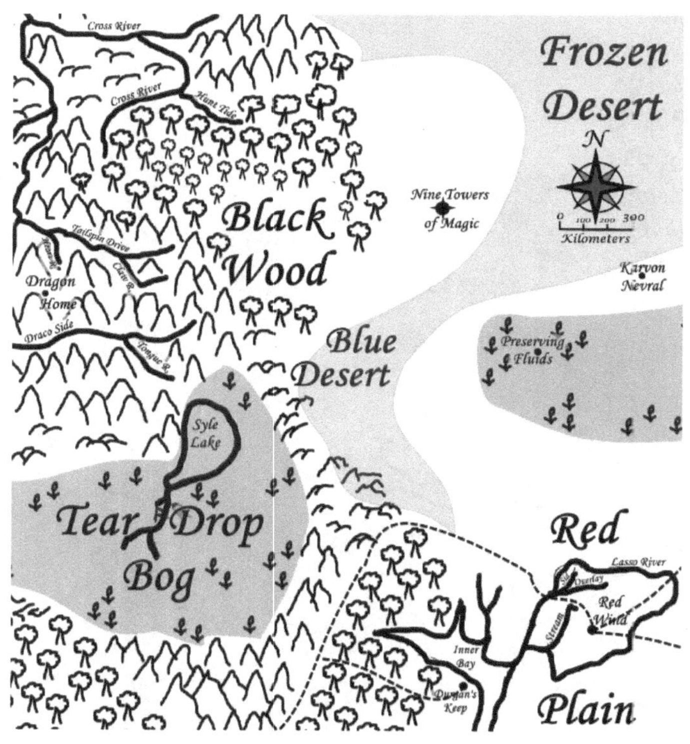
Cross River
Cross River
Hunt Tide
Black
Wood
Frozen
Desert
N
0   100 200 300
Kilometers
Nine Towers
of Magic
Karvon
Nevral
Tailspin Drive
Claw R.
Dragon
Home
Draco Side
Tongue R.
Blue
Desert
Preserving
Fluids
Syle
Lake
Tear Drop
Bog
Red
Lasso River
Overlay
Red
Wind
Stream
Inner
Bay
Duncan's
Keep
Plain

Chapter 1

Torrence fell to his knees in the snow, vomiting onto a spill of his own blood. One arm wrapped across his midsection, and the other was on the pommel of his massive two-handed blade. He supported his weight with the hand on the weapon, stopping himself from falling face first into the muck and mess between his legs.

Covered in gore, chunks of flesh and sinew decorated the blade, and a third of the sword lay embedded in the icy loam of the ground.

Around the weapon lay a half dozen bodies of gnarled men with hyena-like heads. The bodies were hacked and torn, heads crushed, and limbs twisted. More bloody weapons laid around them—broken, rusted, and chipped.

"That'll give you tetanus," Torrence said to no one, "I wouldn't want to get cut by one of those."

But one of those had cut him.

His mind deposited the information into his thoughts, like suddenly remembering where he'd put his keys, or that he had a doctor's appointment on Tuesday. Which he didn't. He'd been driving home from one when he hit the patch of ice.

"That's right," Torrence spoke again, his white fur cloak whipping around him and the wind picking up on the frozen shelf of the mountainside, "I was driving home."

Torrence pushed to his feet, using the sword to leverage himself up. Without thinking about it, he bent and wiped the blade along the still warm corpse of the creature—gnohl, his memory supplied—that he'd killed moments before. The body steamed in the air of the frozen north, and Torrence looked out across the countryside.

He was in the easternmost portion of Ri Steppe, on the western edge of the Frozen Desert. Looking to the south, he could see the Black Wood, a haunted forest contaminated by mages and wizards and sorcerers who'd once occupied the Nine Towers of Magic on its southeastern border.

"What the hell does all that mean?" Torrence asked, his memories gently blanketing him with the information.

It was like remembering a birthday party from your childhood that you didn't even know you'd forgotten. You knew it to be true, but it just hadn't been in your head at all before it was in your head. It wasn't a lost memory that makes you gasp when it showed up again. It was one of those that made you throw up your hand and exclaim, 'Oh yeah!' as you smiled.

The view in front of him, as well as the scene of carnage at his feet, conflicted with the last memory he had of what he'd been doing before thirty seconds ago.

His arm was still across his midsection, covering the vicious wound where a gnohl had almost disemboweled him. A dozen of the creatures had been in on the attack.

They'd dropped stones from above as he trudged through the knee-deep snow. The rocks had fallen around him, and he'd reacted out of instinct, bounding one way and bouncing another to avoid being hit by the makeshift avalanche.

He remembered thinking it was a pemtie idea (pemtie; the word broke his train of thought; he knew it through his body, not his own mind, as stupid or ignorant), and that their quarry—which was him—had a chance of being knocked off the side of the mountain and plummeting far down into the valley below, thus removing the chance for his attackers to loot, or eat, their target.

Then they'd attacked, swarming from hiding places, a half dozen with swords or wicked, twisted daggers. They'd charged him; one being taken out by the final melon-sized stone thrown from above.

The creature had fallen—issuing a brief scream that ended when its head was crushed at the first contact with the mountain side—and then plummeted into the mists below. Torrence had thought nothing else of that one, because it was so far down that even the sound of the body crunching as it hit the ground was lost in the fall's distance.

The others had come towards him, jabbing with their blades, but keeping a distance between them and him. He figured out why as soon as the arrows began coming down from above.

He'd charged the closest attacker—which his current thoughts wanted to call a monster—and used it as a shield. The creature had taken three arrows to the chest before it went limp and lifeless. Torrence had discarded it over the side of the mountain.

As this scene replayed in Torrence's head, he struggled with it because he also had a very different set of experiences in his recent memory.

He had gone to the doctor's, driving himself using the newly installed hand controls in the minivan. It had been nerve-racking, and his thoughts had kept going back to the fateful day where he had lost his ability to stand and walk, his father, and so much all in one car accident. An accident that people told him was no one's fault, just a patch of ice, and that he shouldn't feel guilty about what happened. These things happen, they said.

The chuz they did.

There was another word that had changed, chuz, when he had meant chuz. No, not chuz, chuz. His brain kept translating the loose meaning of his swear words to what his body knew.

His thoughts went back to where they'd been, the difference between the two words fading like a light breeze, unnoticed.

Torrence had been sixteen, and a junior in high school. He was doing well in track and field, football, and soccer, as well as being the favorite of many of the girls. He had only had his real license, as opposed to his learner's permit, for three months when it happened.

A patch of ice, loss of control, a tumbling sensation that included a sharp snapping sound from behind him, and he never heard his father's voice again after those last shouts of panic. He also never walked again.

That meant no more sports, no more girls, no more success, no more friends. He'd been broken, inside and out, completely destroyed.

He'd finished school, mostly at home, through new online courses that were offered in 'extenuating" circumstances.

But today, he'd fought those memories. He'd turned the app on his phone up, blasting music into the small minivan, donated and converted for his use. He sang along, driving and gripping the steering wheel in a white-knuckled grip, and made it safely to his physical therapy appointment.

Though he'd never walk and would be restricted to a wheelchair for the rest of his life, the doctor assured him he was doing well. It was a forty-five-minute drive, a thirty-minute wait; all for four minutes with a nurse checking his vitals, and then three minutes with a doctor that barely looked up from his notes.

The memory jumped, blending with the anger and bitterness of what he was given, what was done to him.

Shunting the thoughts away, he focused on the now, on the present, as he was taught to do when talking to his therapist.

The world lurched. It wasn't *his* world. He was on a mountainside, high above a forest in one direction and plains in another.

This wasn't right.

Where was his car? He had hit the ice, and then he was here.

He stared into the distance, his mind going blank, becoming overwhelmed. The treetops of the forest to the south were still mostly green, but just beginning to get golden, orange, and rust highlights as autumn set in. The snows in the mountains were descending, and in a month or two, it would cover the lands.

Torrence's body took over.

He looked down, moving his arm from the wound he'd received a few minutes ago that ran across his abdomen. It was a bright pink puckered scar now, like he'd visited a healer that wasn't an elder or adept, but instead was just an acolyte that did their best. He shrugged and smiled. At least he wasn't dead.

He lifted his sword, checked to make sure it was clean, swung it overhead with his right hand, caught the tip with his left, and guided it to the leather scabbard on his back. It slid into place effortlessly.

Looking down, he knelt beside the dead creatures and began scavenging whatever he thought would be useful. Rummaging through the gnohls' pouches, he pulled various items out, looked at them and either tucked them into his own pouches, or his knapsack, or tossed them to the side.

He stowed a piece of charcoal, a silver thimble, a bone carving of a bear, and a few other items. Most things were discarded, including stale chunks of bread and crumbly, moldy cheese, rust-pocked knives, and various and sundry odds and ends. The few coins, silver peks and copper fleks, were kept. He held one deep blue gemstone up to the setting sun before dropping it into the same pouch as the coins.

The waning day made him pause. He had to move. He'd been seeking shelter—and keeping an eye out for game that he could use for a meal—when he was attacked. He'd hoped to make the foothills of the mountain before it got too late. He'd seen the glint of sunlight off a stream and had been heading for that, knowing that local fauna would come to it to drink.

Reaching over to a cooling form of a gnohl, he jerked the primitive bow from its massive paw, and wrangled the quiver with a dozen and half rough arrows in it from the creature's back.

Standing, Torrence moved forward. Loping down the path in long strides, letting gravity help him along so he didn't have to put in as much effort, he quickly descended.

He knew he wouldn't reach the bottom before dark, but maybe he could get lucky and hunt on the run.

Torrence's mind picked back up, but cautiously and delicately, not wanting to interrupt the automatic actions of what seemed to be his body now.

He raised his hands, and looked at them—still leaping from the path, to the side of a hillock, to a raised knoll, bounding downward towards his destination in the distance—and saw they were different from his normal mocha-colored skin. These were a brown, but with a tinge of red mixed in. Torrence could feel his long, silky hair bouncing in its braid on his shoulders, instead of his usual tight knit curls.

He was taller than before, and wider, and the weight of it felt different. He thought about that for a moment and suddenly he was in full control of this body.

His feet stumbled under the unfamiliar balance of muscle and height, and he tripped. He went down hard, turning to one side, landing on his shoulder, and sliding two meters in a rain of gravel and sand.

Mentally, Torrence pulled his non-existent hands back from the controls.

The body stood without his help, and he heard a deep, throaty laugh come from it. The head dipped down, the hands sweeping across taut muscles, looking for injury. The knapsack shifted on his back, atop the cloak and sword, and his belt showed his two pouches still attached. The heavy grey woolen shirt had torn, but the woolen pants and leather boots were still in reasonable condition.

He moved forward again, with that easy mountain goat gait, and assured agility that came without thought.

Torrence realized he was in a body. Now, that seemed like an obvious conclusion, but it was more than that. He was in a different body, a body that had an instinctual set of skills. This body took over when he wasn't specifically trying to do anything, and a simple idea of what he wanted to accomplish was suggested, rather than pushed or forced.

He wasn't himself, in a very literal way. He was someone else. Someone who was huge, muscled, and fit. Maybe this was what his body would have been like if he hadn't been in the car accident?

Torrence searched for a mind, any thought that wasn't his own.

He found nothing.

Where was he?

Northeastern Teurone, memories answered, east of the Wandering Hills and Mountains, south of the Ri Steppes, west of the Frozen Desert, and north of the Black Wood.

Torrence fainted in his new head, but the body kept going.

Chapter 2

The Kid picked himself up from the dust of the alley and spun to face his pursuers. His legs should have been broken from the four-story jump he'd made, and he knew he'd blacked out, at least for a moment.

He was a new man, though, and only seconds had passed since he'd jumped. It was like a dream as this new consciousness settled over him, like a new skin over his seventeen-year-old frame.

The bones of his calves knit back together, a surge of otherworldly energy filling his body. With a rush of mixed emotions—from disbelief to wonder, bitterness to hope, and acceptance of the inevitable of the elderly to the endless possibilities of youth—the Kid rose up and smiled.

He, and she, didn't have to die today.

This was the delight of a dream that doesn't feel like a dream, but instead is real. It was the moment most people always vaguely wish for, but never really expect to happen. It was that hope of winning the lottery, getting your dream promotion handed to you, or that other person saying yes to a life and future by your side.

But it was encapsulated by the Kid standing up in an alley.

Fifteen deadly assassins were after him. Rappelling down the sides of the buildings on the thin silk cords of their professions, or just dropping down from windowsill to windowsill until they reached the ground.

But that didn't matter anymore. The Kid smiled, and let out a whoop that even a blind adversary could track him with.

"Talley ho, the game is afoot, Watson!" he shouted.

The Kid ran, joy in every stride, and the thrill of being alive in every action. Laughter, delight, and pure, unadulterated happiness flooded through everything the Kid did.

"Run, run, run as fast as you can," the Kid shouted, "you'll never catch me, I'm the gingerbread man. I ran from the baker and his wife, too. You'll never catch me, not any of you."

He laughed, turning the corner into the main marketplace of Durgan's Keep, skidding around a fruit cart and into the flow of foot traffic of the evening shopping crowd.

Fifteen men and women poured into the street after the Kid. They barreled into merchants and knocked over shoppers, knives gleaming as they ran after the lithe youth.

People dove out of the way, and shrill whistles of the city watch rose in the distance.

The Kid reached a city square, a three-meter-across well on a raised dais in the center, and turned to face his foes. Twin daggers appeared in his hands without him even thinking about it.

The assassins ran into the area, spreading out to cover any escape the Kid may consider. The primary streets, set at the compass points, had two people in front of each of them, and the alleys, at the secondary compass points, had one each.

"This is another fine mess I've gotten myself into, Stanley," the Kid said, laughing, and let his twin blades fly.

One assassin stumbled backwards, clutching at his bloody throat. Another fell forward, a blade protruding from her chest.

The Kid laughed again and leapt from the well into the thinning crowd towards his fallen foes.

Smiling into their fading eyes, the Kid snatched his and their weapons up, crouched and slicing their money pouches free, and dropped them into his own.

The city watch pushed into the building-made valley, cutting their way through the assassins at the edges of the square, allowing the responsible citizens a getaway route. A dozen guards replaced the assassins.

The remaining score of people that weren't involved escaped through the openings made by the patrol, and the guards—stout, tall, and broad-shouldered—formed a human barrier between the Kid and the ways out.

The Kid remembered tales, not from his own memory, but from the memory of the body he now inhabited, tales of the days before the Talisman—the comet that had dominated the sky for so long, raining down its mystical emanations and increasing the power of necromancers and summoners everywhere—of when Durgan's Keep wasn't a refuge for people attempting to get away from the demons to the southeast, or the constant trickling influx of undead from the west.

Once upon a time, Durgan's Keep was home to adventurers and merchants alike. Founded by an intrepid rokairn, Durgan, he laid out plans and sectioned off an area of wilderness to create a balanced trade town that grew into a fortified capital of the eastern part of the continent. His aeifain and other companions each put in their thoughts about what their own race would like in a section of town, and after twenty years of construction, Durgan's Keep was born.

The demon invasion of almost a hundred years ago—long before the Talisman—as maniacal beings from other dimensions flooded out of Land's End to the southeast, was the herald of change. It had started a series of events that included the now infamous necromancer, Rondarius the Foul, escaping from his multiple-century-long imprisonment.

Then, when the Talisman stopped in the sky and stayed, hanging over the land for decades, everything went to shit.

The Kid hadn't been around for that, in either form.

That thought made the person at the core of the Kid pause and consider. But then the rush of the guards and assassins allowed the Kid to stop thinking and throw himself into action.

He ran forward and leapt into the air. His feet caught nothing, but he continued to rise. The guards beneath his boots, bent suddenly as if they had been trampled over, though the Kid's boots were almost a meter above their heads.

The Kid flipped, spinning heels over head through the air and catching onto the walnut windowsill of a third-story apartment.

The surrounding architecture reminded the person inside the Kid of the Tudor era of their own world. Dark wood boxing in and slashing across walls, beige plasterwork was the dominant style. A fair amount of stonework balanced it, showing the craftsmanship of the rokairn builders of Durgan's Keep.

Pulling himself up, the Kid saw a woman's face with her mouth in a moue of surprise staring out the window at him. With a wave of his hand, he drew on the energy of his mind and touched hers.

"Hocus Pocus, baby," the Kid let out a cat-like yowl, and changed.

The woman now saw a cat, struggling outside her window, trying to pull itself up and angry people below pointed at it with raised crossbows and readied throwing blades.

The woman reached forward and shoved the window open, before scrambling backwards to avoid the flurry of daggers that struck the window frame outside and the bolts that hit the ceiling within.

She saw the cat leap inside, yowling, as the Kid ran past her, shouting a thank you to the woman.

He ran through her sitting room, threw open the door to the hall, and stopped to listen. Angry voices came up from below, and the sound of booted feet on the stairs echoed hollowly.

The Kid ran up the last flight of stairs. A square opening showed the sky outside of the stairwell. He clambered out of the window frame at the top of the stairs. His fingers grabbed unseen holds, and he pulled himself up the outside of the building. Looking down into the alley ten meters below, the Kid saw a tall, thin assassin with carrot orange hair leaning against the wall with his arms crossed, watching him climb with a dull disinterest.

It was Mezk the Damned. Well known for his pact with demons, people whispered he'd agreed to let them have his soul when he died, but he would never die of violence or injury.

How could I know this about someone I've never seen? The Kid thought, and his grip on the wall slipped, and he fell.

He caught himself on the window he'd climbed out of, and pulled himself upward, focusing on what he was doing, his heart pounding, rather than random thoughts about what he should and shouldn't know.

Once he gained the rooftop, he was on his way to escape. Using his magics, he pushed himself with each leap, allowing him to jump spaces two or three times wider than a normal thief could jump. With a nod and a wave, people forgot he'd just passed their window, or just didn't see him at all.

Life was grand.

Or at least it was until he settled on top of the peaked roof of a Church of Jonath. Sitting with his back to the warm chimney, his legs bent, and his butt resting on the slate shingles of the stout building, the Kid wondered about his death.

"Jonath's trident," he swore, using a phrase from the memory of his body.

He knew he'd died. He'd fallen four stories off a roof, landed on his feet, and broke both legs. Falling backwards, he'd caved in the back of his head in the cobblestone alley. But here he was, alive and well, but not the same as he was before.

He also knew that his other body, in a different world, laying in a bed, dying of stage four cancer.

He knew he had all his skills, all his knowledge, and even his memories for the most part, but he also had more. He had a second set of skills, knowledge, and memories.

These other memories were foreign, but at the same time felt more real than the roof on which he sat. They held decades of life; including a husband who'd left her; a son who died in a coma of liver failure because of alcohol poisoning when he was just a month from graduating college with a doctorate; and a plethora of skills, ranging from cooking fried foods to knitting to how to write a resume in Microsoft Word.

The Kid remembered he was once been called Jen, but that was a world away, even a lifetime away. None of that mattered anymore. He was here, and he was loving life.

No more, he thought, pushing any other memories to the side. He was the Kid now, and belonged here. This was his body now, and this was his world. And he would live life to the fullest this time. No more worrying about what was right or proper, or what the boss thought of her dress, or if that man in the street wanted to hurt her for the couple of dollars in her purse.

She would miss Cuddles, her Pomeranian, but the nurses would see to the dog.

He would, the Kid chided himself. He would. He would no longer be she who was, instead he would be him.

The strange thought swirled and bumped around the Kid's head. With a chuckle and shrug, he brushed the thought aside.

Standing up, he looked across the rooftops, watching twilight settle in. The low hanging cloud of smoke from wood fires cooking dinner and warming houses in the late evening filled the sky just thirty meters above the city.

He had been on a job, but it had been lost in translation.

"Que sera, sera," the Kid chuckled again, "whatever will be, will be, the future's not ours to see."

With a quick twirl, the Kid straightened up and ran for the edge of the rooftop, threw himself off, grabbed a canvas awning below to pull himself to it, bounced off it, and flipped to the street below.

Why didn't he ever think of doing things like that before tonight, he wondered as he sauntered up the street, happily whistling.

Chapter 3

Esperanza staggered backwards, away from the crowd of strangers, reaching for her adoringly. They were all talking at once, some weeping, some screaming, and others just whispering. But all seemed grateful to her, and the words 'miracle worker' were being repeated over and over.

The dark-haired woman tripped over the hem of her long robe, her hands flying up as she fell backwards. She landed hard on her butt.

Holding her hands out in front of her, her sleeves sliding up her arms and pooling in the crook of her elbows, she stared at the blotches of grey and brown fading from her skin. Swollen and puffy flesh shrunk as she watched, veins receded to normal sizes, and capillaries healed as bruises disappeared under her gaze.

A second set of impulses, almost thoughts, flooded her mind, pushing the fear and surprise aside. They told her of the power of Latress, goddess of wind, weather, and wisdom. Mother of the twin gods, Torr and Tarra, and wife of the god of justice and earth, Jonath.

The thoughts told her of the favor of the goddess, and how it had blessed her and would shelter and protect her, and how it had guided her in healing the hundreds of sick people in this village, saving them and their children from being wiped out by the plague.

Esperanza shoved the thoughts away, pushed at that other identity, and screamed, tearing at her own hair, pulling a fistful out with each hand.

The crowd stopped. They stared at her uncertainly, not sure what to do.

One middle-aged woman stepped forward, holding out a hand, and said something in a language that Esperanza thought she should comprehend. But it wasn't English or Spanish, and though she felt she knew it, her mind blocked out any understanding because it was impossible.

The woman approached like most people approached a scared and wounded animal; cautious, slowly, speaking gently, and making comforting noises between words.

The woman came close enough to touch Esperanza and knelt as she took the younger woman's hands into her own.

Esperanza fainted.

Esperanza woke in a small room. She put a hand above her head, and it bumped a wall before she could even extend her arm all the way. She could see the wall at the foot of the bed by the faint light from the dim fire in the ceramic chiminea that stood beside the door, to her left and barely more than an arm's length away. Smoke curled from the top of it, drawn out of a hole in the mud wall. Directly across from the door was the only window in the room. Woven reeds of twisted branches created a shutter placed over the opening, then covered with a thicker blanket to keep the chill outside, and the heat inside.

Esperanza ran her fingers along the wall beside the bed, on her right. Under her hands, she could feel fibrous plants mixed into the clay to help give the wall strength. The whole place smelled faintly of must and dung, the latter from the dried horse manure that burned in the chiminea.

Rolling onto her left side on the burlap mattress filled with reeds, Esperanza saw her few possessions on a table of woven branches. It held the holy symbol of Latress, a gusting cloud with seven stars around it. Subtle etching seemed to show a face within the cloud. Beside it was her herb pouch on its thin leather belt, her neatly folded robe, a few hair combs, and a small mortar and pestle.

And a small knife in a sheath.

She picked up the blade and drew it from the holder. She stared at it.

She had been ending her life, and now she was here. This knife held her eyes as it moved along her forearm and wrist, as if of its own volition. It scratched her skin, leaving a white line in the flesh.

"Latress's Breath protect me," she muttered, wondering at the words she uttered.

That wasn't *her* God, but it felt like it was the one watching over her right now.

A rough curtain hung in the doorway and the smell of something cooking drifted from the other room. A woman's voice sang a gentle lullaby, more humming than singing, and the sound of wooden bowls and utensils clunked against each other.

The sounds stopped when Esperanza sat up, the bed creaking and rustling underneath her.

"Hello?" the woman's voice said from the other side of the curtain.

Esperanza could see a form through the opening between the wall and the hanging barrier. It looked up and to one side, giving her guest the courtesy of privacy.

"No," Esperanza muttered.

"Oh, you're awake," the woman pushed through the curtain and smiled down at her guest, "maybe you'd like to freshen up?"

The woman had a coarse clay pitcher and large bowl in her hands, and she set them on the small table beside the bed. She pulled a rough cloth, tucked into her apron strings, out and set it beside the other things.

"There's a chamber pot and scrapers under the table," the woman smiled down at her, "and just come on out when you're done."

Esperanza came out ten minutes later, looking traumatized.

The room she stepped into wasn't much bigger than the bedroom, and only had one door that presumably led to the outside.

The woman looked up from her squatting position in front of a fireplace. She was stirring some sort of stew in a ceramic pot that sat directly on the hot coals of the fire.

The rest of the room was plain. A table with two chairs sat on one side of the fire, and a low wooden bench covered with blankets was on the other side. Esperanza guessed this served as a couch, but also the woman's bed, while Esperanza was her guest.

Directly across from the small knee-high hearth, which was a brick and mud affair, was what Esperanza guessed was the kitchen. It wasn't more than a few shelves set into the mud walls with supplies neatly lining them.

"Everything come out okay?" her hostess asked, smiling and showing a mouth with missing, broken, and brown teeth.

Esperanza just stared at her as if she hadn't understood the words coming out of the woman's mouth.

"Well," the woman stood, "I'm guessing it did, otherwise you wouldn't be out here. I'm Rose, by the way. I thought you may have remembered it, but considering everything you've just gone through, it must have addled you."

Rose moved to get wooden bowls from the kitchen area, and Esperanza looked at the woman.

Rose was younger than Esperanza originally thought, at least twenty years younger, and probably in her mid-thirties, which would make the woman less than ten years older than herself. Rose must've had a hard life, and was slightly bent as she moved about the house, her grey streaked hair in a tight bun on her head held by a blue ribbon, and her knuckles swollen and red from hard work.

The decor in the house was somewhere between simple and nonexistent. Curtains of faded yellow hung over the one shuttered window, and a painted urn with a large chip from it stood on the table to hold drinking water. Wreaths and braids of dry herbs hung from the ceiling.

Rose squatted next to the hearth to spoon out some stew into two shallow bowls. She stood, groaning, and brought the bowls to the table and set them down. Taking two ceramic cups from the shelf, she set them on the table also, and filled the vessels with cloudy water from the painted urn.

"Sorry, we don't have no beer," Rose smiled sheepishly, showing her broken teeth, "or any meat with all the animals dying. Hard to make these things when so many in the village were too sick to work, or died from the plague. But that'll all be changing now that you've fixed things."

Esperanza thought that the woman would be pretty if she wasn't raised in a third-world country. Then she wondered how she'd gotten to this place, and why everyone spoke English here.

But it wasn't English, nagged some logic in the back of her head. She could understand Rose, and all the other villagers earlier, with no issue. But it wasn't any language that she knew, except her brain did know it. Like a reflex, it just caught the words, and she knew the meaning with absolute clarity.

"Come on, then," Rose waved at her, then gestured to the second chair, "you gotta eat, right? Even a priestess needs to eat, at least as far as I know."

Esperanza moved to the chair, pulled it out, and sat. It was a high ladder-back wooden chair with a woven straw seat, and surprisingly comfortable.

Rose unwrapped a loaf of dark bread, tore a hunk from it, and set it on the table in front of Esperanza's bowl. She repeated the process for herself before wrapping the bread back up and setting it aside.

The bowls were small, and the hunk of bread was about as large as your average dinner roll. Looking around, Esperanza realized that this was everything they had to eat, and it was probably more than most of the villagers had on their tables tonight.

That was when Esperanza realized she hadn't seen anyone who was overweight here. She'd seen people who were sickly thin, perhaps because of the illness the village had suffered, or perhaps because of the food shortage Rose mentioned. It could've been a combination of the two.

"Latress's rains bless this food," the words came out unbidden by her conscious thoughts, "and nourish us…"

Esperanza stopped, looking up at her hostess, who was smiling, then looked back down.

Esperanza picked up her wooden spoon, dipped it into the dark brown broth in the bowl, fished out a chunk of potato, and raised to her mouth. Sniffing without realizing she was doing it; she smelled the pungent aroma of peat moss. That was the musty smell from earlier also, she realized.

With the tip of her tongue, she tasted the stew, if you wanted to call it that. It was bland and thin, but had a faint meaty flavor of mushrooms.

Rose was watching her expectantly, smiling supportively as she ate. When the woman saw Esperanza looking back at her, Rose raised her spoon in a toast and then slurped her broth from it. Esperanza looked at the woman's shallow bowl and saw that there were no potatoes in it.

Esperanza remembered her grandmother, the woman who had raised her. The woman had only spoken Spanish, but found a way to get a job and keep food on the table, clothes on Esperanza's back, and the water and power on. And she always made sure that Esperanza had a nice dress, new shoes, and the portion of dinner that had meat.

When Esperanza questioned her grandmother why she never had any meat, her grandmother explained that it was too hard for her to chew, and she didn't want any. When Esperanza was older, years after her grandmother had died, she'd realized the truth. The woman always made sure her granddaughter had the best that she could give her, even if it meant that her grandmother went without.

Rose, sipping at her broth and watching Esperanza with her potato-laden spoon, suddenly reminded Esperanza of her grandmother.

Esperanza smiled, put the potato in her mouth with the wash of broth, chewed, made appreciative noises, and nodded at Rose.

Within minutes, the two had finished the meal. Esperanza wanted a glass of water to rinse the dirt from her teeth—the water from the urn was clouded with it—but she only showed appreciation.

Rose chatted as she cleaned up, telling her guest how everyone was doing everything she'd taught them, even boiling water before drinking it, washing things twice, and cleaning their hands before eating or sleeping.

Considering the hanging herbs, and things Rose said about teaching the villagers specific things, Esperanza had concluded that Rose must be something like the village's wise woman. And the woman did seem to care about everyone's well-being.

Something thudded against the shutter from outside, and the smell of smoldering flame rose. Through the cracks in the shutters and the front door, they could see dancing orange light. Shouts began filling the night, and within seconds screams followed them.

Rose rushed to the door and pulled it open. Over her shoulder, Esperanza could see the slow, shambling forms of the walking dead.

"Give us the damned witch," a deep voice boomed, "or I promise each and every man, woman, and child in this village will join my rotting army."

Rose looked back at Esperanza over her shoulder.

"Bring out the priestess of Latress or everyone dies," the man's voice shouted, louder and closer this time, "and then will be brought back from the dead to serve me for eternity."

Chapter 4

Torrence crouched in the underbrush, bow held across his bent knees, with the quiver at his feet. He watched the slave train through the thicket of thorny bushes. The guards were setting up camp for the night, shouting at the chained prisoners to build campfires and other menial tasks.

The banner on a staff showed the slaver's mark and the caravan's personal symbol, a wolf head in a red circle. This was the Blood Sun Wolf slavers then, and memories of stories of their trade floated through Torrence's head. They were known for selling to anyone, for any purpose, and weren't known for their kindness or quality of stock.

Though part of him knew that slavery was common since the Downfall, he wasn't really on speaking terms with that part of him. Being in this body was like moving into someone else's house moments after they'd left it.

Things were just lying around, waiting to be used. Thoughts, memories, and innate skills honed through years of practice. Like how he'd heard the wagons, and before he realized what he was doing, he'd hidden in the underbrush. Or like last night, he'd drawn and nocked an arrow, raised the bow, fired, and killed a rabbit before he even knew he'd moved. Instincts took over if he relaxed and just knew what he wanted to do.

Slavery wasn't cool though, everyone knew that. He'd learned about it in school and heard about it all his life. Not that he'd ever known, met, or even heard of someone who'd been a slave during his lifetime; but he did know that his ancestors had been slaves.

The bottom line was that you can't own another person. He didn't even like dudes or chicks who were overly possessive of their other half, hanging all over them and blocking other people from talking or hanging out with them. He didn't like bosses that treated employees like crap, and he really didn't like bullies.

Torrence sometimes wondered if some of the kids, when he was in high school, had thought he'd been a bully. He didn't think so, though. He knew he'd picked on a few kids, but they'd practically begged for attention, and all in the wrong ways. The spazzes and freaks that liked to talk shit when they should have just shut up.

But it wasn't like he beat them up. That would've been ridiculous. Usually, they went away with a cross-armed stare, or a little verbal encouragement. And he did have that nerd friend back in the day. He'd looked out for the kid because he was okay. He didn't talk shit, even though he was smart.

After the accident, Torrence had dealt with the other side of the coin on occasion. Never directly, no one would ever pick on someone in a wheelchair where others could see. But sometimes, he heard the people laughing. Or he'd see them notice him as he was approaching a door, and they'd let it close even though he was almost to it. People ignored him more than anything, acted like they didn't see him trying to get something off a high shelf at the grocery. And the ones that did and helped him often had a look of pity.

Torrence didn't know which one bugged him more.

Why can't people just chill the chuz out, and be cool? He thought. *Treat others decently, without making it feel like some heroic act of kindness. Was that really so hard?*

"Work harder," a harsh voice yelled, "we don't want to get caught by the night without fires set, you dirty lazy bastards!"

"Yes, Master Dropsum." The answering voice was snarky and mocking. "We wouldn't want you to get eaten by any scary monsters, would we?"

"I'm the scary monster," shouted the first man, apparently the guy who ran the caravan, Dropsum.

The sound of a whip, followed by a ragged gasp, brought Torrence out of his thoughts.

He stood up, nocked an arrow, and fired. Just like last night with the bunny—and thank goodness this body took over when he needed to clean and cook it— he'd reacted after having nothing more than an impulse with no thought.

Seventeen men stared at the arrow sticking out of the hand of the man who had held the whip a moment before.

The fat man—who was clutching his bloody and pierced hand—widened his eyes, crouched slightly, and let out a whining shriek that started low and slow, and raised in pitch and intensity. When the sound hit its apex, he jumped up and down, screaming as much in rage as in pain. After a couple bounces, he stopped, gasping. He renewed his scream as the pain of making the arrow that stuck through his hand wobble and jiggle when he jumped, struck home.

A thin man with shaggy blonde hair and a bloody whip streak across his chest crouched in front of Dropsum and looked at Torrence with keen interest.

Master Dropsum's snapped his head to one side and made eye contact with Torrence. All heads slowly turned towards the source of the arrow.

Torrence smiled sheepishly and shrugged.

All hell broke loose.

The men, as one, drew weapons. Swords slid from scabbards, daggers from sheaths, crossbows came up, and spears were leveled at Torrence. Many of the three dozen slaves dropped to the ground, tucking their head between their knees, and covering them with their arms.

Panic flooded through Torrence, and he shook, trying to decide if he should run or hide.

His body took over.

His arms came up again, the left holding the bow, and the right pulling arrows from the quiver. One man dropped with two arrows in his chest. Another man took one to the knee, ending his career as a guard, and fell to the dew moistened dirt of the road. A third took a superb shot to the eye, and his head jerked backwards, and his body followed.

The rest rushed towards Torrence, who was frozen in fear, unsure what to do. But his body knew, and it dropped the bow.

"Jonath's trident!" Torrence shouted a war cry, but thought to himself, *Why the hell did I drop the bow? I was doing so good with the bow.*

Torrence was already moving forward, whipping his two-handed sword from the scabbard on his back, and swinging it in a wide arc. Three men had taken the lead, one in front of the other two. The sword met the man's body where the neck joins the chest, and the collarbone crumbled under the power of five kilograms of steel.

The sword twisted, and the flat of the blade hit the man in the side of the head. He crumbled underneath the blow, and Torrence spun the blade, using its own momentum, and brought it back in the other direction.

The two men that had been right behind the first skidded to a halt, holding their blades in both hands directly in front of them. The return route of the barbarian's enormous weapon, as he fell to one knee, brought the steel under the men's pommels and into their forearms.

The thing about two-handed swords is that they're not made for cutting. You can hone their blades, but more often than not, they're more of a large steel club with a flat part. They crush things as much, if not more, as they cut things.

The power of the muscle behind the blade shattered the first man's right forearm and spun him. His blade shot to his left as his arm crumbled, the point dropping and stabbing into the groin of his companion. The remaining man of the opening charge not only took his buddy's sword tip to his junk, but also had the follow through of the huge barbarian blade to contend with, and it dragged itself across the man's throat. His windpipe simultaneously crushed and torn open.

The remaining eight men—not counting the guy near the slave train trying to decide if he should pull the arrow out of his hand or not, and looking more than just a little, like he was about to cry—formed a circle around Torrence.

Torrence had a grip. It was a double-handed grip on his massive sword—and he snickered as the thought, if you know what I mean, crossed his mind—but it was also a grip on the situation. He was in it now, and he wasn't getting out of it until he'd handled it. So, he set his feet, and his mind, and readied himself for whatever came next.

Of the eight men, four had spears, three held daggers ready to throw, and the last was a gigantic man who swung a massive double-headed flail in a lazy circle at his side. Two more guards hung back, crossbows at the ready.

The spearmen stepped forward, jabbing with their two-and-a-half meter long weapons to keep the barbarian centered. The men with the daggers, in unison, drew their arms back and prepared to throw.

Torrence didn't think. Well, he didn't plan his next move, but thoughts shot through his head when he realized what was going down. The men had created a crossfire. This could be bad for him, unless he made sure that they missed him. Then they could, and likely would, hit one of the caravan guards on the other side of him.

Torrence smiled.

"You know, guys," the barbarian said, "if you run now, and pray to Chanian for speed to get away, you might live."

Torrence didn't know who Chanian was, but as he thought that, the information was there. Chanian was a god. Like a superhuman being that people prayed to for blessings in a certain area. Chanian happened to be the one who people prayed to for speed in travel, guile, agility, and stealing things.

This made Torrence think of moments earlier when he'd sworn and said, 'Jonath's trident.' Jonath was a god of Justice, and the element of earth. Guards and farmers favored him.

Hm, Torrence thought, *that's kinda like Mars from the Roman mythology. He was a god of war. But not many people knew he was also the god of agriculture.*

Torrence snapped back into awareness of the present moment. He apparently had ducked under a couple of flying daggers, grabbed a thrusting spear and pushed it behind him into the gut of one of the other guards. He'd also dropped his own sword, grabbed that guy's spear and spun in a circle, hitting three of the men in their heads with the thirty-centimeter blade of the appropriated weapon.

Four of the eight men in the circle were nullified in a couple of heartbeats. Three held gushing cuts on their heads, and the fourth was stumbling backwards with his friend's weapon buried in his intestines.

That left four more.

One of those didn't have his spear anymore and had two daggers stuck in him, one in the torso and another in his foot. He stumbled out of the circle, which had quickly dwindled to a triangle.

The slaves who hadn't dropped to the ground—and instead had crouched, ducked behind a wagon, or just stood stock-still to see what was happening—began shouting and charging towards any of the guards still standing. The two crossbow men went down first from their efforts, taken by surprise from behind.

Dropsum, caravan master—the fat man with the arrow through his hand—was overcome by the lithe blonde man. The slave, followed by the slaves connected to him by ankle chains, grabbed the man's hand and shoved it towards the slave master's own face. The two toppled into the dirt, rolling around as desperation for survival played out in front of the others.

The second chain gang ran to the wagon, pulling those slaves that had dropped to the ground along with them, and started grabbing anything they could use. A few grabbed water skins or food, but most had more foresight and grabbed things they could throw at their captors or use as a weapon.

A half-dozen of the people attached to the man who had attacked the caravan master joined in the activity of beating him down. The rest looked around, saw the triangle of men facing off with their rescuer, and charged in that direction.

In less than a minute, the guards were either running into the surrounding trees, injured and surrendering to the superior numbers of the slaves, or lay dead on the ground.

Torrence turned away as prisoners rejected the surrenders and offered the guards a second option of being brutally beaten to death with the slaves' chains and bare hands.

Why does it bother me that the men were being beaten to death? Torrence embraced the thought to keep his mind off the sounds of the murders behind him.

He'd just killed a dozen men in combat without thinking twice about it. *Was that so different? And didn't these people deserve a chance to exact some revenge for what they went through?*

This was a cruel and pitiless world, and Torrence walked away from the sounds that spoke of that in the plain language of violence.

Once out of sight, he turned back towards the caravan and wondered what else this day would bring.

"Where's my body right now?" he whispered, his stomach twisting. "Am I dying, or dead, and this is my brain dealing with me fighting for my life?"

Chapter 5

"This's the Kid," a gruff, accented voice said as a finger jabbed into the Kid's shoulder, "and he's been doing bad things. Things like stealing, then giving it to people who didn't earn it. I have big plans for this town, and that kinda bidj ain't gonna cut it."

The Kid looked up at Jakdin, a third-rate thug for the Grey Ash gang, and focused on the man's broken nose with a scar running across it from his right cheek to his left eye.

Jakdin had been trying to make a name for himself lately and had been shaking down a lot of the street kids who actually worked for a living. The man wanted to rise within the ranks of the organization, but never seemed to get anywhere.

"Standing on the backs of people who actually do the real work again, Jakdin?" the Kid asked, smirking up at the man who stood over him.

The four toughs who always accompanied Jakdin rumbled laughter, and their leader glared around at them.

"I heard you had a run in with Mezk and some of Bokk's other men," Jakdin went on, ignoring the comment, "and that you led them into a trap set by the city watch and ran off with the score."

"Shit happens, y'all," the Kid said with a shrug, looking around the Open Door, a local dive of a pub.

It was a busy night, and the place was filled with mercenaries just returned from the Demon Front, a war zone to the southeast where people fought to keep the visitors from another plane of existence from overwhelming the last of human civilization.

Durgan's Keep, the walled city that sat on a cliff overlooking the Inner Bay, was one of the last places where men could live without fear of the constant threat of attack by demons, undead, or monsters. It had once been a thriving place; full of merchants with wares from far-off lands, travelers with tales of wonder and adventure, a mix of races that brought diversity from all over, and a solid feeling of safety from a government that worked hard to keep it all moving.

Now, it was still a pinnacle of civilization, but the events of the last few decades tainted it. A dark miasma of greed and cruelty had fallen over what was once a strong and fair place. People were as likely to slip a stiletto between your ribs as sell you the rack of lamb hanging in their shop.

The Open Door once greeted visitors, showing a taste of the city that was beyond it. Now, it was a grungy, dank place frequented by corrupt city guards who weren't much better than the criminals that they drank with.

"You gave it away," Jakdin said plainly, "you didn't even make a profit and pay your dues to the guild. You just gave it to dirty, stinking losers who live off the scraps. I don't get you, kid."

"It could be because you have a tiny brain," the Kid wasn't looking at the man anymore, instead his eyes shifted around the room because he knew the inevitable was coming, "and you can't see beyond what's right in front of your beady, little pig eyes."

Jakdin's fist smashed down on the table, cups and bowls rattling and bouncing with the blow.

The pub quieted, people looking towards the corner table where the Kid sat.

The Kid had seen Jakdin coming, had even known he was on the way. He was observant, and people on the street liked him and fed him good information, mostly. The Kid had a point to make, and swallowed a lump in his throat, wondering if it was a good idea to do this.

Sighing, the Kid leaned back and looked up at Jakdin.

"Is this worth dying over?" the Kid asked. "Do ya feel lucky, punk. Well, do you?"

"Maybe you should ask yourself that," Jakdin sneered.

Smiling, the Kid flicked a peanut shell onto the ground, and it skidded across the floor and under a table.

Jakdin and his thugs turned to watch it land.

A form, not much larger than a cat, clattered out from under the table where the shell had disappeared. It had eight legs, hair bristling on each one, an orangish carapace with razor sharp ridges, and two massive claws that clacked as it scurried towards the feet of the thugs.

"Sebastian," the Kid said confidently, "kill the boy."

The mutant crab ran at the men's ankles, one claw snapping at one thug. The man screamed as his foot was clipped from his leg.

The pub exploded into chaos.

Barmaids leaped onto tables, regulars dove behind the bar, or ran up the flight of stairs that led to the rented out rooms above, and even the burly men-at-arms from the demon front danced backwards, away from the creature.

Jakdin screamed in surprise, a high-pitched noise that caused more than one person to stop looking at the creature on the floor and stare at him.

The broken-nosed man leapt onto the Kid's table, drawing his sword—a wavy blade, like a Kris blade but three times as long.

With another gesture, the Kid unlaced the man's boots with his mind and caused the cords to intertwine with one another.

Jakdin danced around on the table, still screaming shrilly, and toppled off because his laces were tied together.

His sword skidded along the floor and disappeared into the crowd.

The Kid, now on the other side of the room and grinning, bent down and retrieved the blade.

"Thanks for the souvenirs!" the Kid said, holding up five coin pouches in one hand and saluting with the weapon in the other, as Jakdin scrambled backwards on all fours to avoid the charging creature. "I'll make sure I pass it on to some undeserving folks."

The Kid darted into the kitchen and out the open back door into the alley. Pushing with his mind, he leapt to a second-story window, pausing to deposit a half dozen gold kords—the twisted golden wires that were the local currency—that he'd taken from the coin purses of the thugs on the sill, and tapped on the window.

He pushed off again into the open air, reaching out with his mind to the opposite wall, and flew across the alley to a third-story window, and repeated the depositing of gold kords and tapping on the window.

One final leap and he pulled himself onto the rooftop.

He knew the illusion of the little monster wouldn't keep the men in the pub busy for long, especially once he'd moved a short distance away. But it was enough to embarrass the brutes publicly, and he got a sword and some loot in the deal.

Bonus!

The rooftops were the Kid's own private thoroughfare, and he moved across the city unseen and faster than if he'd taken the standard routes people traveled.

Once he was closer to the docks—his actual destination—he dropped into another back alley and casually entered the foot traffic of the street.

It was after dark, but commerce and trade were still booming here in the red-light district, even at this hour. Women and men of all sizes and shapes called out to passerby, offering pleasures of the flesh for coin.

Sweet Jewlnee called out and waved at the Kid. She was an immense woman, with a mountain of red hair coiled and piled atop her head. Her makeup was a riot of color. The rouge splashed across her cheeks, eyeliner outlining her emerald eyes, and a rainbow of eyeshadow filling out the space in between. Her silk sari of blue and gold contrasted with her kerchief skirt of a dozen different dyed silks.

The Kid smiled widely and veered through the crowd to the woman that his memory told him had taken care of him many times. Not in the romantic way, though that offer was always on the table. Sweet Jewlnee had given him a warm place to sleep on cold nights when he was just a lad, fed him buttered rolls when he had nothing else to eat, and was one of the few people that always greeted him with open arms instead of a closed fist.

"Sweet Jewlnee," the Kid said, "flower of beauty and royalty of the night mists, how are you?"

"Oh, you," Sweet Jewlnee blushed and opened her arms to take the boy into her embrace, "I'm better now that I've seen your smile. And, how're you?"

The Kid fell into her soft, warm, encircling arms, and was smothered against her ample bosom. The heavy perfumes she always wore washed over him, and even though it threatened to make him sneeze, it was a smell that brought back pleasant memories and always made him smile.

She grabbed him by the shoulders and pulled him away to arm's length, staring into his face.

"You're going away," she gasped, "you're leaving Durgan's Keep!"

"Oh, Sweet Jewlnee," the Kid's smile spread across his face without any effort, "you always could read my mind, and the minds of others. Guess that's the secret to your success?"

"That," she said coyly, "and a few of my other talents as well. But yes, the same magics I saw in you, and schooled you in, also tell me many secrets others don't need to say aloud. But, why are you leaving? Are those men being mean to you again, sugar plum?"

The Kid laughed, hugged the woman again, and then pulled away, his fingers running down her arms until they were holding hands.

A heavy pouch clinked as he transferred it from his hands to hers. Her eyes shifted towards it and then darted back to his.

"What's this?" she asked.

"A gift," the Kid's voice was tight with a fleeting moment of emotion, and he paused before going on, "for your kindness. Share it with those who need some of that kindness for themselves, but make sure you keep enough to get yourself something pretty."

She leaned back, looking at him through slitted eyes.

"You need something," she laughed.

"I didn't come here to ask you for anything," the Kid said with sincere innocence, though he blushed.

"I didn't say that you came here to ask me for anything," she smiled a gentle smile that spoke of wisdom and knowing. "You *need* something. And I can help with that."

The woman inside of the Kid felt a reaction. The kindness of this madam; this woman of the night— who had lived decades in a dark and cruel world—was offering something, not because someone asked, but because they needed it, and her heart wanted to help.

Jen, the Kid thought, *I was Jen, and I remember being kind, and having kindness from others who wanted nothing in return; like my first boss, or the pro-bono lawyer who handled my divorce, or Angie who was my best friend, or the nurses who answered my call bell.*

The thought fell away, like the passing memory it was. But more of Jen blossomed within the Kid, and he teared up.

"I don't know what you mean," the Kid's voice was strained and choked, "I don't want anything."

"I know, honey pie," Sweet Jewlnee said, "and you never need to ask. I know a guy at the dock, Jaimin Rabbit. He's a real prick, but he's also one of the sweetest assholes I know. He'll make your stomach turn with his annoying damned puns, but he'll help you. Go and ask for him. His ship is the Raptor Rex, it's in dock now."

The Kid leaned on the railing of the Raptor Rex, wind in his face and gusts making his dark shoulder-length hair dance. The ship moved across the midnight waters of the Inner Bay, cutting through the waves and breeze to the north, away from the Ruled River that led south to the ocean.

A young sailor, pale with a mop-top of red curls, named Jundek, was polite and offered to show him knots and when and where mess was eaten.

The rest of the crew avoided the Kid, except for an older man named Tillheim, who watched him, nodding when the Kid helped on the deck, or frowned when another sailor made a crude comment.

He didn't remember much else of the trip from the red-light district to the docks. He had a vague recollection of moving through the streets, dropping coins into beggars' cups, hats, and plates, and handing silver peks to children and anyone who looked like they'd put in a hard day's work and wouldn't earn that much in a week.

He'd lurked in the docks, searching for the ship called Raptor Rex, only to find it docked out in the harbor. He'd rented a skiff and a boatman to taxi him out to it. The man called Jaimin Rabbit had listened when the Kid told the sailor that Sweet Jewlnee had sent him. The Captain tossed down a rope and plank ladder, told him to come aboard, and shooed the taxi back to shore.

The Kid didn't know what awaited him to the north, but he did know that this world was full of adventure. He also knew this world needed a helping hand to find more than just the spoonful of misery that it normally dosed to its people.

65

Chapter 6

"This can't be happening," Esperanza muttered, her hand fingering the blade on her waist, "this isn't real."

Rose's pale face reflected the torchlight of the burning brand that had hit the hut and threatened to set the moss-and-mud-covered walls ablaze.

The woman stared back at Esperanza, wide-eyed and indecisive.

Esperanza wanted to wake up. She knew she'd taken too many sleeping pills with the pint of vodka, and might never wake up, but this wasn't the heaven or hell she'd expected in death.

Could she end it right now, using the small blade she gripped? She didn't belong here. It wasn't real.

Everything felt real.

The smells filled her nose, the sounds met her ears and didn't have that thought quality of a dream that noises had when sleeping, and she felt genuine emotion instead of the impression of it when unable to wake up.

She'd only felt fear since being here. The crowd coming at her, waking in a mud hovel with no bathroom, even the dirty water that Rose had presented as if it was the finest wine, was terrifying.

Now, a man called for her head. If she was, in fact, the priestess of Latress.

She was Christian, not some unknown heathen witch of some fake religion. She'd always prayed to God in Heaven, and never even considered other faiths of people who didn't know of Christ and his works.

But here she was, watching half-rotted corpses shuffling through a village in the night. She saw one grab a man who jabbed at it with a wooden pitchfork. Its hands were fleshless and skeletal, tearing at the villager's face and throat, ripping away chunks of flesh as the man fell, screaming, under the onslaught.

Three others, what could only be called zombies, shambled to the struggle, and fell—literally fell, as in dropped face first—onto the man and began tearing out ribbons of flesh and biting into his stomach, arms, and face, choking back the bits of skin and muscle they'd torn free.

Esperanza stumbled backwards, wondering what kind of private hell God had sent her to for her sins.

A thought, a feeling, a voice in her soul pushed at her, urging her to step forward and call upon the winds, the storm, the rains, and the lightning. To call down the very forces of nature to strike down the abominations outside.

Esperanza fell to her knees, screaming and clutching her head in hysterics, her voice calling out to God, Jesus, and the angelic hosts to come save her. She sobbed the Lord's Prayer, only wanting this nightmare to end.

She clutched her knife with one hand, and the holy symbol of the Goddess Latress with the other, not realizing she'd done it.

Through tear-blurred vision she watched as Rose—who'd turned to stare at her—was grabbed from behind and dragged into the night by decaying grey arms, skeletal fingers questing for the woman's throat.

Esperanza froze.

The only person since she'd been here that had been kind to her, cared for her, and showed any understanding and patience…was now being dragged into the dark by an unearthly terror.

And Esperanza couldn't even stand up.

Something popped, like the snap of fingers deep inside her, and she was in the backseat of her own body.

Esperanza stood, rising with confidence that hadn't been there moments before. Releasing her small blade and the holy symbol, she strode forward, through the door and out of the mud dwelling, into the night.

She raised her arms, striding into the midst of chaos and horrific death, and called upon her Goddess.

"Latress," she said in a normal tone, but her voice boomed like thunder and echoed off the surrounding dwellings, "grant me the wisdom to face this foe with knowledge of their weaknesses, and your power and might, delivered upon them as holy wrath!"

Lightning arced from the dark clouds above, shooting with a blinding flash to Esperanza's outstretched hands, and then darted in a dozen directions to strike the living dead that attacked in the night.

"Latress," Esperanza intoned, turning slowly, a holy glow surrounding her, "light the night, and free these good people from the evil that threatens to consume them!"

Orbs of magical light zoomed from the priestess and flew in slow, lazy circles throughout the village. The undead creatures lurched away from the light, seeking the shadows and murk.

Esperanza saw Rose beside the hut. One of the grey creatures bent over her and four more moving towards her struggling form.

"No," Esperanza said calmly, but with an intensity that even the dead couldn't ignore.

The decaying forms turned towards her.

She took three steps forward, gripped the metal holy symbol of the clouds and stars—which she'd thought she'd left in the small bedroom, but now hung around her neck—and raised it in front of her.

Holy power, that was the only way Esperanza could later describe it, filled the area. A calm in the storm weighed on the village, and the people nearby stopped running, stopped screaming, and instead drew deep, grounding breaths. And then the pulse of energy burst forth from the symbol.

All the dead creatures that stood, walked, shambled, lurched, or moved in the path in front of her—widening as it went—slowed, turned, and faded. Their skin became translucent, and their bones within their broken bodies began to shine. The power of Latress filled them, and they hesitated for a moment, and then were pulled away as dust in the wind. Their forms dissipating like the nightmares they caused in the waking morning light.

Rose sat bolt upright. But her face didn't show fear. Instead, her eyes were ablaze with something Esperanza had never seen. She stared at Esperanza with hope. Faith. Belief. Confidence that she, Esperanza, would make all the bad things go away.

The priestess of Latress, that was Esperanza, turned away from Rose and moved to continue her personal holy crusade of eradicating the undead menace.

Rose was not offended; she saw the powerful woman who'd come into the village almost a month ago to help them with an affliction they couldn't battle alone. A woman who contracted the same diseased infection that she was saving others from. A woman who'd died last night. Then, as suddenly as her own death, had risen again, a scared and confused stranger that used a different name. But now, the priestess that had saved them all strode into the forces of darkness that had descended upon the village.

"You, witch!" the powerful male voice tore through the night, "I've come for you, and you shall die for what you did to my master, the Overlord of Death, Knight of the Darkest Night, Lord of Rot, and Regent of Revenants, Philibert the Foul. He was forever wiped from this plane of existence and banished to eternal suffering with the demons of the netherworld by your hand, and I shall return the favor upon you!"

Esperanza turned her head to glance at the ranting man. He was of average height, a bit rotund, and slightly hunched, with thinning hair. He wore a leather chemist apron, the same kind that many blacksmiths wore, but with less pizazz. It was stained with various splotches of chemical mixtures and compounds.

She stopped, cocked her head as she turned towards him, and looked at him with a mixture of bemusement and curiosity.

"This is your doing?" she asked. "This is your little army of undead?"

"It is," the paunchy man sneered, his unkempt hair whipping around his head in the wind, "you whore-slut of an impotent goddess!"

"Oh," Esperanza said with a laugh, "I remember you!"

She turned and walked towards the man, looking at him askance. With each step she took towards him, he took a half step back, and she slowly closed the distance between them.

"I also remember Philibert," her voice grew in power, and a crescendo of thunder rumbled in the air with each sentence, building each time she spoke, "he was a sad little man who intimidated others to make himself feel better about himself."

"I, Louis the necromancer, proclaim you a liar!" the man shouted.

"Really, dude?" a bit of the real Esperanza burst through for a moment. "Don't you guys have a clue about the value of a decent stage name? I mean, even J-lo would be more intimidating than Louis. Isn't that the name of the nerdy loser from Ghostbusters?"

"Ghosts!" Louis screamed, clenching his fists in front of him as he backed away from the approaching priestess, "will haunt you, devour you, and destroy your soul."

"You really don't have a clue, do you?" Esperanza asked. "Do you really think I have anything to fear from you? Don't you remember what I did to the man who taught you a third of what he knew?"

"A third?" Louis asked, his voice cracking.

"You were the one hiding behind the bunk beds when I fried your boss with lightning, bestowed upon me by my impotent goddess, weren't you? You were crying, right? That was you?"

"No," Louis mumbled, stumbling over a tree root as he backed away, and falling on his ass, "I wasn't crying. I was…"

The man hesitated.

"I was," he continued, his voice picking up strength again, "having trouble seeing because you blew up a bunch of alchemical supplies, and it burned my eyes!"

"Oh," Esperanza sighed, a gentle rumble of thunder echoing her breath, as she reached up and took hold of the holy symbol of Latress that hung between her breasts, "I see. So, the sobbing and all that snot as your master roasted to a crisp was because of some fumes that hardly bothered me, a whore-slut, at all?"

"Yeah," Louis mumbled, "I have allergies."

"Louis," she said menacingly, drawing out the vowels in the man's name like a disapproving teacher, "I think we're done here. I'm going to make it so your creations want you, but in a very different way than they did when you created them."

A burst of wind lifted the man a handful of centimeters off the ground and then dropped him unceremoniously back onto his ass.

The breath woofed out of him, and he let out a grunt of surprise.

Villagers had gathered to watch the confrontation, standing in clumps near the front doors of their huts, ready to bolt back inside at any sign that the priestess's efforts were in vain.

The dozen or so undead that had lurched into the protective darkness of the trees from Esperanza's light globes now reemerged and shambled towards their master. They were silent except for the sound of their feet sliding over the mat of dried leaves on the ground.

Louis looked up at them in surprise, a look that quickly changed to triumph. He pushed himself up to his feet, rising to his full unimpressive height, pulled his shoulders back and made his gut seem even larger, hiked up his drooping drawers, and thrust his doughy chest out.

"Yes," he breathed a throaty growl to his minions, "come to me, my children, come to your master!"

The emaciated figures limped towards him, their hands reaching for him.

He smiled and brushed his fingertips against theirs.

"Now," his victorious tone spoke of his impending victory, "go and destroy everyone so we may replenish your ranks! Then we shall travel to join Aku'ji and combine our forces with her army of the night!"

The pathetic creatures, not much more than bare skin and bones, crowded around him, grabbing his hands, his arms, and leaning into him.

"Yes, yes," he said, the confidence in his voice being replaced with confusion, "I know you love me; I know that I'm the best..."

His words disappeared in a surprised cry of pain.

"You bit me!" Louis whined, "You chuzzing bit me, you ungrateful brainless bastard!"

His voice rose with each word, and then cut off suddenly, replaced with a strangled gurgle, his body collapsing under the weight of his adoring, but eternally hungry, minions.

The creatures collapsed on top of the amateur necromancer as his life force slipped away, and the power and control he had over them dissipated. He died under their loving onslaught, and the magic he'd empowered them with left them as his last gasp left his body.

Esperanza let out a breath she'd been holding since she'd been put into the backseat of her own body. She was back in control of herself, and the instinctual drive that had led her to the actions over the last handful of minutes disappeared. Her eyes went wide when she began to understand what had just happened.

She turned to look at Rose and the other villagers, and saw they were all coming towards her, their faces unreadable.

Travis I. Sivart

Chapter 7

Torrence cleaned his sword and stowed it on his back.

A few minutes later, the sounds of the fight died, as did most of the caravan guards, replaced by the sounds of chains being thrown aside, wagons being looted, and people running off into the woods by themselves or in small groups.

Torrence went back to the caravan and was stunned by how completely it had been dismantled in such a short amount of time. A few people still rummaged through the remaining rubble, stripping boots or gear from dead guards, or just standing and staring as if they didn't know what to do next.

The newly freed prisoners avoided Torrence, darting past him and giving him a wide berth. Two or three nodded or muttered thanks, but didn't stick around to see if the stranger would try to put them back into chains.

The light-haired, wiry man who'd attacked the caravan master looked up from a chest of various spices. He was stuffing a burlap sack with the smaller bags and satchels of rare herbs and seasonings. He wore the vest and boots of the man who Torrence had put an arrow through the hand of.

The man, Master Dropsum, had dragged himself away from the carnage, and Torrence could see the heels of the man's bare feet sticking out from under a bush about five meters away.

"Thank you," the smaller man stood, squared his shoulders, and looked Torrence straight in the eye, "thank you for my life, as well as the lives of all the others."

"Um, yeah," Torrence realized he wasn't speaking English, but talking in a language his body knew and understood, "no problem."

"Why, though?" the man smiled, cocking his head like a curious dog. "Why would you do something so pemtie as attack an armed slave caravan? Are you trying to get yourself killed? Or was the woman you love, one of the prisoners?"

The man looked around to see if anyone seemed to recognize his rescuer, or if the big man seemed to know anyone here. The small man shook his shaggy head.

"Um," Torrence wondered the same thing himself, "it seemed like the right thing to do?"

The smaller man laughed and shook his head again, kneeling back down to stuff more spices into his sack.

"That sounded like a question," the thin man said, "but whatever your reason, I owe you my life and I'm grateful."

Pausing, the man looked up at Torrence.

"I'm Axle," the blonde man stood, wiped his dirty hands on his thighs, and then stepped towards Torrence with one hand extended.

"Torrence," the barbarian reached to shake the man's hand.

Axle reached past the barbarian's hand and grasped Torrence's wrist, shaking it as Torrence imitated the movement.

"Torrents," Axle said, "well, it fits your fighting style, that's for sure. You were a force of nature. You didn't pause or give a second thought. You were damned impressive, my friend."

Axle released Torrence's wrist and stared up into the big man's face, smiling.

A man and woman moved past the two, leaning on one another as they headed into the tree line. They nodded and muttered their gratitude without making eye contact, and shuffled away.

"Can I offer something in return for your heroism?" Axle asked. "You don't look like you're looking for a slave, so I guess I could offer my services if I can do anything to repay you."

"Your services?" Torrence was unsure of what that would even mean.

"Hm," Axle looked at the barbarian, "perhaps you're simple, perhaps you honestly don't expect anyone to show courtesy or kindness in this day and age."

Torrence shrugged.

Axle moved about the abandoned caravan, looking for anything the other slaves had missed before their exodus. He found a short, pocked blade in a worn leather scabbard. Pulling a belt from one of the dead men, he wrapped it around his waist and tucked the weapon into his waistband.

He stopped and looked at the barbarian again, his head cocked.

"Where you headed, Torrents?"

The big man shrugged again.

"How about this," Axle squared off in front of Torrence, "I'm going to go back to my village, Hope's Hollow. These guys caught me when I was outside of it, cutting wood. You see, I'm a woodsman and a carpenter. I make great wagons and carts, with the proper tools, if I can brag for a moment. And I'm going to go back home. My village was suffering from a plague, but a priestess of Latress showed up and helped. I expect that she's dead now, because when I was taken about a week ago, she was showing signs of the sickness herself, but she'd done a lot to help stop the spread of it while she was there. Why don't you come with me?"

"Why?" Torrence was unsure of what else to say.

"Well," Axle smiled his amiable smile again, "I'll be honest, it's for strictly selfish reasons I ask. You're a big guy, and can obviously take care of yourself, and I'd feel safer traveling with you instead of by myself. You don't seem to have anywhere in particular you're going, so Hope's Hollow is as good a place as anywhere else."

Torrence shrugged again.

"It's settled then," Axle began loading waterskins and loaves of bread into another burlap sack, "we'll travel together to my home, and see what happens from there."

"Do you think they made it?" Torrence asked.

"Who? The other people who ran off into a place called the Black Wood just as night was falling?" Axle looked at Torrence over his tin plate of beans and bread. "No, I think they were total pemties and were probably dead before sunrise. Did you notice how few corpses remained the next day? Something got those and probably got the living as well."

The two men ate in silence for a few moments.

They'd traveled together for three days, heading west along the foothills of the Wandering Mountains and the northern edge of the Black Wood. They'd spent the first night in the ruins of the caravan, building a small fire to cook over and then keep warm with the glowing coals in the night, but avoiding attention from predators.

There'd been screams, but Torrence had hoped it had been something mundane, like a screech owl or the haunting call of a fox. This was the first time he'd asked about it and regretted it immediately.

The second day was uneventful, besides a brief encounter with a territorial badger who'd hissed and gruffed at them when they came too close to its den.

Today had been different, though. The pungent smell of rotting bodies, lots of them, had reached their noses. By the time they'd decided to make camp, it was even stronger.

"What do you think that smell is?" Torrence wiped at his mouth with a small cloth.

"You know you're the tidiest damned barbarian I've ever seen?" Axle asked in return.

"Don't avoid the question," Torrence said, then turned and spat, as if to disprove Axle's observation.

Axle laughed and bent back over his plate.

"How far are we from your village?" Torrence tried to strike up conversation again.

"Probably a week from where we started," Axle said without looking up, "but it could be more if the dragons are out."

"Dragons are real?" Torrence asked.

"Well, they were," Axle answered automatically, then stopped and looked up at his traveling companion. "Was that a real question? Where have you been? Before the Downfall, the Wandering Hills were home to an entire clan of them. They kept humans the way we keep sheep."

"For food?" Torrence's eyes were wide, and his spoon had stopped centimeters from his mouth.

"Maybe," Axle shrugged, "but more likely to tend the herds of cows that have much more meat and breed quicker than people do. And to bring in more gold and stuff for their hordes."

The wind shifted, and the smell of rot came into their small campsite stronger than before. It wasn't the smell of a dead predator; carnivores had an almost earthy smell when rotting. It also wasn't the smell of an herbivore, which was rather mellow and gentle unless it baked under the hot sun for a while, and even then, it was an eruption of aroma when the body burst open from the pressure. This was different. It had a taint, not quite a chemical smell, but as if a cesspit had been covered with rotting flowers.

Torrence interrupted his own thought flow, wondering how the hell he knew all this. It's not like he'd Googled it. That meant that his body must have had enough experiences with the death of animals, mild and wild, as well as people, to know the difference between their dead smells.

Suddenly, the meaning behind that occurred to him and he sat bolt upright, his eyes wide.

"Gas?" Axle smirked.

"Dead people." Torrence's voice was much calmer than he thought it should be.

"What?" Axle spun around and looked into the shadows of the surrounding trees. "Do you see them?"

Torrence laughed at the memory of a movie from his past and again thought that sort of behavior shouldn't be normal. Did this world have zombies and vampires just moseying around and waving at folks? Was it such a common thing to see undead, like in so many movies and TV shows, that his current body didn't even react with fear, shock, or surprise?

Realizing he'd stood up, and had his huge two-handed broadsword—Torrence also realized he knew what the hell a broadsword was, it was also known as a bastard sword and was able to be used in a one- or two-handed grip—at the ready and was in a battle stance.

The weapon was held in his right hand, just above head level, and extending at an angle in front and across his body as he bent at the knees for easy movement when he needed to strike. It was a defensive stance, waiting to see the enemy's position and intention. It would allow him to swing overhead for a powerful strike, drop the weapon into a thrust, or drop his hands and the pommel to create a block, which in itself could be shifted left or right, depending where an attack came from.

A glance over his shoulder showed Axle standing behind him, across the fire; both faced outwards into the darkness, letting their eyes adjust to the shadows that the light of the fire had intensified. The smaller man held the sword he had liberated from the well-looted caravan in his right hand, and a long, thin dirk in his left.

The night moved and shifted, and pale shapes coalesced in the dark. Dozens of lumbering forms came into view, and one dark shadow, low and feral, darted forward.

Chapter 8

The Kid had left the Raptor Rex three days ago—Captain Jaiman Rabbit had explained to him it was called disembarking—and had traveled north of the Inner Bay, crossed the road that had once brought merchants and travelers from Red Wind in the Red Plains to the east to Dioneze City and beyond to Runsk in the Diaz Woods, south of the Tear Drop Bog in the west.

He had traveled alone, staying in a small village full of suspicious people the first night, then sleeping in a hollowed-out tree the second night, and under a deadfall the third.

The fourth day had brought rain. A cold, dark storm with torrents of weather that limited vision when he entered the foothills that were bordered by the Tear Drop Bog—a salty swamp that had once connected to the ocean—on the west and the Blue Desert on the east. The desert was named because its sands had a blue tint to it from the magical runoff of mystical experiments of the Nine Towers lost in its northern reaches.

The Kid pulled his cloak tighter around himself and wished, not for the first time, that it reached to his ankles instead of ending just below his waist.

He trudged along the small path, not much more than a deer track, on the foothills between the bog and the desert.

His feet slipped, the ground crumbling underneath them, and he fell into darkness. Landing, his head hit something hard, and his vision swam.

When it cleared, he wasn't sure if he'd passed out or not. He lay amongst dozens of stone blocks in a cloud of dust that was dissipating in the moist air of the drizzle that came in through the opening five or six meters above him.

He breathed out a heavy sigh, and reached to rub the lump on the back of his skull, wincing as he touched it.

Dim grey light filtered in from above. Looking up, he could see the opening that he fell through.

"What the hell am I doing?" he asked aloud.

But that wasn't him, that was his body asking, which was a strange concept, as if he were two people, but one was all reaction and instinct, and the other was a conscious being.

"I am me," the Kid said, pushing away the other part of him that didn't seem to delight in being on an adventure.

That was the part that would've never attacked Jakdin, never left Durgan's Keep, and never wanted to explore this new and amazing world that waited for him.

Why had I left? he wondered.

The answer was obvious to one part of him, because there was so much more to life than one city. But the other part of him argued against it, pointing out that it was almost guaranteed to be full of unknown dangers.

"Chuz that," the Kid said aloud, standing and brusquely brushing the roots, dust, and muck from his clothes, forcing the reactive side of him deep down inside, "Life is meant to be lived, and to refuse to go out and experience it is a sort of passive-aggressive suicide."

But to go out and experience is a direct path to death, an almost certain thing, said the distant voice inside before it disappeared in the motion of stepping forward into the darkness.

The Kid swooned and touched the bump on his head again, his fingers coming away wet with mud and blood. He dabbed at it with his cloak and realized that wouldn't be enough.

Pulling a small canteen from the woven hemp bag over his shoulder, he poured some water on the scrape, shrugging away the thought that he was dribbling water down his back. He was already drenched from the rain anyway, what's a little more water matter?

He steadied himself on the worked stone wall with one hand, waiting for his eyes to adjust to the gloom. While he waited, he inspected his surroundings.

The hole above was three to four times his own height above him, and the fallen stones around him wouldn't be enough to stack and make his escape from… where was he, anyway?

He looked around; his eyes having adjusted.

He stood in what appeared to be a hallway, extending into the darkness in one direction. Behind him, under some stones, was a wooden bench with holes in it, each about thirty centimeters in diameter, and the musty smell of old feces hung in the air.

"I fell into the shitter?" the Kid asked out loud, and then yelled, "Shitter's full!"

The sound of his own voice echoed back to him from down the passageway.

He giggled.

"The dog peed on the sandwiches!" the Kid shouted the quote to no one, and laughed even harder.

"I decree this place," the Kid said in an official voice, "the Griswold Tunnels, and claim it for my own! I shall raid and loot, and possibly die if I don't find a way out, through this place in the name of adventure and fun!"

The Kid moved a couple meters forward to get out of the rain falling through the hole in the roof, knelt, set his satchel down, and rummaged through it. After a few moments of searching, he found an oil lantern, a metal flask of oil, and a flint and steel.

He found it fascinating to watch his own hands work of their own accord, as if on autopilot. They poured a small amount of oil into the reservoir of the lamp, capped both the lantern and the flask, pulled up some oil-soaked wick, lit it from a spark of the flint and steel, and then spooled the extra wick back down into the lantern's reservoir.

He stowed all the items in their proper places around his body.

Standing up, the Kid slung the bag back over his shoulder and neck, and moved forward and down the hall of what he thought of as catacombs. The Kid had never been in catacombs, in either life. It felt very Edgar Allan Poe and the Cask of Amontillado. Maybe something from National Treasure or one of the Boris Karloff flicks from the Kid's childhood.

The dank, sweet smell of rotting vegetation and of things that dig in dark places hung in the air. The ground was moist with dust that had settled and become a sludge over the ages, and the Kid's boots squelched with each step.

The hall turned to the right. The dark behind the Kid swallowed the light, and the dim illumination fought its way into the inky blackness ahead. The patter of rain falling into the crumbled hole faded into the distance. The thick sound of silence enveloped him, only interrupted by his own footfalls, the creak of leather, and the rustle of cloth from his own gear.

After walking a dozen meters, he came to a four-way intersection. The Kid crouched at the juncture, tilting his head one way then the other, listening for anything to break the silence.

Pushing his hand into his satchel, he pulled out a small leather pouch and drew out three stones. Tossing one to his right, he listened to the echoes of it as bounced along the floor. The moisture wasn't as thick here, and the dust wasn't muck. Instead, it was a slightly damp carpet.

The rock to the right click-thumped down the hall. The Kid closed his eyes to listen for subtle differences in its path. The echoes that came back spoke of a long hall with some openings on either side. The left hall returned almost identical results. The Kid waited, listening to see if he had disturbed anything.

In movies, the Kid remembered, catacombs and tombs always had rats or bugs in them. Which was odd, since nothing within a long abandoned and dead place could support an ecosystem of scavengers.

Nothing moved, at least nothing the Kid could detect. He laughed, the sound echoing off the surrounding stone, his mind inventing things in the dark, shuffling towards him on feet silenced by the layer of detritus of time.

He tossed the third rock forward, closing his eyes to listen. That one thumped gently across the same soft surface covering the hard floor and then clacked on less covered stone floor, the echoes speaking of a large chamber ahead.

Yes, the Kid thought, *come forward and free me.*

But it wasn't the Kid's thoughts. Maybe it was a thought from the body he now inhabited? But no, it didn't feel like that, either. He laughed again at the boogie man he'd made up in his head.

Standing and raising his lantern, he turned left and moved in that direction. Small alcoves appeared in the gloom to his left and his right, dust raised by his own feet dancing in the light, and he stopped to inspect the nooks.

The openings were only about an arm's length deep and were dominated by a statue in each. The figures were humanoid, but also reptilian in small ways. The one on the right seemed to have pebbled skin, and the one on the left had no hair, but a raised crest along its head and down its neck instead.

Behind each statue was a square stone, about a meter in height and width, with a plaque embedded. It was an internment chamber, as best as the Kid could tell. The writing on the plaque was not a language the Kid or his body recognized.

Each of the six alcoves in this hall was similar, though the statues each showed different reptilian mutations. Tails, claws, scales, snouts, and other features decorated the forms of ornately carved marble, and the Kid guessed that these were the heroes of some long dead species or culture.

At the end of the hall was a larger alcove, almost twice the size of the others. The statue within it was a curled dragon, its head raised as if watching the hall, and ruby eyes staring into the darkness. The Kid felt that this was a scaled—no pun intended—down version of the actual creature it represented.

He debated if he should attempt to pry the gems free. On one hand, no one had been in this tomb for a long time, he guessed, and it was unlikely that anything would object to him taking what was just lying around. On the other hand, he didn't really have any great urge to desecrate what was so obviously a work of art.

In the Kid's previous life—a memory pushed at her as who she was bubbled to the surface—she remembered visiting museums and wondering in awe at art and artifacts that were thousands of years old. She also recalled her trip to the pyramids and ruins in central Mexico, the Pyramid of the Sun, and the Pyramid of the Moon at Teotihuacán. She remembered being sad, even angry, that people had raided and looted the grand treasures that had once decorated those stone halls.

Good, the voice said, snapping the Kid back to the present. *You shouldn't take those. They belong here.*

The Kid shook his head, laughing at his overactive imagination. But he followed the advice, backing away from the statue before turning to explore the other hall. He moved across the intersection and found similar alcoves, statues, and burial plaques there.

Returning to the intersection once again, he turned to his right towards the chamber that had echoed in a way that spoke of open space. He moved towards it.

The room opened in front of him, and the light of the lantern spread across a space larger than the circle of illumination.

The Kid saw a double handful of wooden pews to the left and right, a second set on the other side of the room mirrored the first from across an aisle. People lined the benches, deteriorated clothes hanging from gaunt forms that had decayed in the moist air. Empty eyes stared at the center of the room.

In the middle of the chamber was a raised dais with a single step circling it. Floating in the air above it, dust motes dancing around it, was a lone, white-bladed dagger.

The Kid moved forward to inspect it, and the congregation with hollow dark stares stood as one and turned to look at him.

Yes, the voice said in his head, *keep coming, pay them no mind, liberate me from my prison.*

As the Kid turned to look at the dagger, it gleamed, a dull light emanating from it.

Chapter 9

The shadow moved faster than Torrence could track, darting across the clearing and disappearing into the trees as the slower, lumbering forms shambled into the circle of firelight.

The undead that came forward were fresh, as in they weren't decayed and dried husks. Instead, they were still moist with the remnants of life and bodily fluids. They jerked and shuddered with each step, as if some remaining piece of who they'd been fought against the black magics that animated them, commanding them to seek the living, and bring them into the dark fold of a necromancer's siren call and control.

Axle didn't wait. He darted forward, bringing his weapons to bear. Knocking a groping, atrophied claw-like hand of the closest walking dead away with his thin dirk, he slashed out with his sword and cut along the belly of the tortured creature. Intestines wetly fell to the ground with a splattering noise, pouring onto the man's boots and entangling his feet as he darted to his next target. Tripping on the entrails, Axle went face down into the dirt.

The creature standing over him wailed, a breathy, pained sound that didn't come from the wounding it received.

The other dead thralls echoed the noise, and Torrence thought their suffering didn't come from fear or injury, but instead came from the horror of their remaining consciousness being forced to do things they would have never done in life.

Axle rolled to his back, stabbing upward into the thigh of another, what Torrence could only think of as, zombie. The weapon embedded itself into the bone, and the creature's step faltered as it looked down on the prone, and easy, prey at its feet.

Torrence had been watching his new friend and guide. He'd forgotten to watch for his own safety. A dozen hands grabbed at the man, pulling him to wrinkled, dehydrated lips and mouths with blackened and loose teeth.

A shadow hissed from behind the things grappling Torrence, and it almost seemed to hold a voice, and a meaning, in the noise.

Torrence raised his weapon above the arms gripping him, changed his hold on the blade, and brought the sword down and across the limbs in a swift motion.

The weakened grips broke free, throwing the things sideways with the strength of the movement.

"Aku'ji," a voice hissed from the trees.

Torrence looked towards the noise in time to see the sinewy form of the lightning-quick beast springing at him.

The thing barreled into him, knocking him backwards, and he stumbled over the small campfire and fell onto his back.

Torrence lifted his legs from the flames and rolled out of the fire. The thing from the trees still atop him, and held back from tearing into his face with pointed teeth by the sword.

The barbarian pushed upward with his weapon, one hand on the pommel, the other on the blade, at the same time as he bucked his hips and threw the thing away from him.

The creature weighed almost nothing, being barely more than bones, sinew, and skin. Its head was devoid of hair, and its face contorted in a rictus of hate and anger, as if the constant pain it felt was only held at bay by killing and feeding.

It flew off the swordsman, rolled, and leaped back into the shadows of the trees.

Buried under the impaled creature, his sword—embedded in the thing's thigh bone—ripped from Axle's grasp. His dirk flashed, once, twice, three times, and cut ligaments and tendons on the monster's neck, back, and thigh, the man moving his attacks lower along the body.

The creature still writhed, but with the puppet strings of biology severed, it had little to no control over its own body.

It, thought Axle, pushing the thought forcefully into his own mind. In actuality, the thing rolling off him looked like a plump, middle-aged woman that had smiled at him in his village's marketplace as he traded a few coins for a push-barrow, just three months before.

He blinked away the thought and rolled to his feet. Grabbing his pock-marked sword, he waggled it from the thing's thigh, shoved his booted foot into its gut, and pulled his weapon free.

Three more dog-piled on top of him, pushing him back into the dirt. The shadowy form of the lithe undead leaped on top of the mound of fighting forms and swiped downward with its clawed hand, hissing.

"Aku'ji," the thing rasped, clawing at Axle's eyes.

Would an undead without eyes before it was turned be less efficient? Axle wondered, squirming his dirk along the midsection of one creature, and pulled the weapon free, cold innards spilling across him.

Claws raked across the blonde man's forearm.

Axle plunged the blade into the bloated eye of the thing above him, pulled it free, and did the same to a second.

Torrence pulled his sword free from the body of the fifth undead creature to attack him. Body parts, still squirming and twitching, lie around the tortured torsos at his feet.

The big man spun towards his friend.

Axle struggled under three of the bloated dead; two of them clutching at their ruined eyes, and the third attempting to get to him by biting its way through the other two zombies. The ghast—Torrence's mind supplied the word—perched on top of the whole pile.

"This is some bullbidj," Torrence said, and swung his sword in a wide arc.

The blade met the rasping creature's neck, snapping it with an audible noise. Knocked three meters with the blow, the thing scampered away on all fours and into the trees, its head bouncing back and forth from its chest to its shoulder.

Torrence skewered the topmost zombie, flinging it aside, and kicked the next one from the pile.

Axle thrust the remaining creature away, rolled to his feet, slipped in the loose, wet slurry of guts, and stood, weapons at ready.

Sounds of labored breathing from the two men, sibilant gasps from the undead monsters, and the noise of the retreating ghast filled the clearing.

Axle stabbed downward, piercing one of the undead's eyes and pushing his blade into the brain. The monster went still. He chopped at the thing's neck, severing the head, and kicked it away from the body.

"Take their heads," Axle panted, "then we burn them to make sure they can't come back."

"Yeah," Torrence said, "I know that."

And he did. He knew it twice. Once from his own world and the books, movies, and TV shows that made up the mythology of the living dead, and a second time from the memories of the body he now wore.

The two made quick work of the remaining creatures, all the while keeping a watchful eye for the ghast or more of the newly made dead.

Nothing else came, though they both agreed that it felt like something was watching from nearby.

They piled the heads, after removing them from the bodies, into the fire, adding the wood they'd collected to keep the fire going.

The odd combination of wet corpses and dried extremities caused the fire to alternate between sputtering and flaring, and the two men gathered more wood as needed, always staying together.

Their clothes were wet with ichor and juices from the newly dead things, and the smell clung to them. Unlike many smells, they didn't get used to this one, and a shift in the wind often caused them to gag as the odor hit them anew.

Once they'd tossed heads, limbs, torsos, and other odd bits in the fire, the two gathered their few belongings and headed into the night.

Three days later, they arrived in the small village of Hope's Hollow. It was just after midday, the sun hidden by looming clouds that had an odd orange tint to them.

The only other encounter the men had in their journey was a two-headed bear that fought with itself as much as it snapped at them. The beast seemed to have grown it recently, they surmised by the ripped and torn flesh from which the extra head had jutted.

When arriving in the village, three men armed with mauls and pitchforks greeted them. Recognizing Axle, the men hailed him with caution.

"Axle," an older man with steel colored hair said as he nodded, "where've you been?"

"Caught by slavers outside of town, Richeal," Axle smiled at the man and rested his hand on the pommel of the sword at his waist, "got free with the help of this lug."

The three men eyed the barbarian, taking in his size and weapon.

"Torrents, this is Richeal, Frebel, and Bert," Axle said, gesturing at each man "gentlemen, this is Torrents, a swordsman of some skill, a tracker of beasts, and slayer of the undead."

"Hm," Richeal grunted, then gestured past him, "well, go on then. I think your hut is still standing, and no one's moved into it yet, but I can't guarantee that people haven't taken what they needed from it."

"Excellent," Axle bowed to the man, and then strode forward as he turned to Torrence, "at least we'll have a roof over our head tonight."

"So," Torrence followed Axle, "I want to call bullbidj on you being just a woodsman and a carpenter."

98

Travis I. Sivart

Chapter 10

The Kid felt torn between running for the dagger hanging in mid-air before him, or turning to face the three score skeletal forms moving towards the center aisle between the rows of pews. They walked in slow, jerking steps towards him in a single file line, like parishioners moving towards the front of a church to take communion.

He ran forward, leaping into the air as he reached the first step of the dais, and felt a tingle along his skin when he entered the area surrounding the dagger.

Awareness washed over him. The feeling of being entered filled the Kid. His mind reeled as a presence intruded and layered atop his own.

He stood in an empty chamber, identical to the one he'd been in moments before. Differences lit up in vision, like how hidden objects in children's shows or that old TV series, Psyche, would reveal themselves to the characters looking for clues.

Things popped into existence, one at a time, then moved with life and motion.

The room was lit with glowing orbs of magic, casting clear white light across the immense chamber. The pews were bustling with believers; the passageway behind the Kid—that he'd just come through—was plainly visible and showed an inscription above it that said 'Hall of Heroes'. A passage to the right led to the chamber being excavated for guests, priests, and visitors on holy pilgrimages. Across from it was where the attendant priests and acolytes were housed, and showed people grouped together, laughing and talking. The two remaining halls that led to the outdoor area of worship were wreathed in fresh boughs of holly and mistletoe.

The parishioners were of many more species and races than just human. Towering people with reptilian heads prayed, short and stout rokairn mingled with lithe and graceful aeifain and dasism, and other peoples of all skin tones peppered the crowd.

A half dozen priests, resplendent in silk robes of reds, yellows, and oranges interwoven with threads of silver and gold, discussed topics, and waited in the wooden choir box for the ceremony to begin.

Then the ground shook and dust sifted down from the ceiling.

The Kid was back in the present, landing on the dais, his hand outstretched to grasp the weapon floating in the dim gloom of the chamber. His lantern had fallen from his hand in the jump, crashing to the ground and shattering. The oil, scattered on the temple floor, caught fire and small flames dotted the path the Kid had taken.

The gaunt figures were closer, and a humming rose from their forms that no longer had lungs and throats to raise such a noise.

The other vision returned.

Priests encircled the platform, hands and voices raised in prayer and supplication, as the worshipers in the room were slain by thin creatures with enormous eyes and green or grey skin. Demons ruptured through glowing orange portals, cutting down anyone within reach with swords of flame and smoke.

The Kid was again in the now, his hand closer to the blade. His fingers hit a barrier that pushed him away from the artifact.

Don't quit now, the voice encouraged him, *you've almost got me.*

The world spun in a swirl of colors, and the vision swelled again.

Four reptilian beings in robes stood on the dais, one at each of the cardinal points, chanting. A fifth priest lay on the altar in the center, holding a silver dagger in one hand and a large, curved tooth, the size of his own forearm, in the other.

The room beyond was awash with blood and gore. The head of a dragon—the Kid instinctively knew that's what it was (what else could be that large and scaly?) but couldn't fathom how it had gotten inside the underground complex—lay jutting into the room from the side passage that led to the priest's quarters, its mouth bloody where a tooth had been torn free.

The voices of the four priests rose to an apex, the walls shook, and the altar crumbled. The fifth priest, on the stone table, pulled the silvered weapon and the dragon's tooth together, and stabbed them as one into his own chest.

The stone he laid on, his body, and the weapons fell into themselves, collapsing into a coalesced singularity.

The four chanting holy men's words cut off, and they screamed, but that cut off as well. A silent, unseen burst of energy rushed outward and threw the demonic and green and grey forms backwards.

Then the room was silent.

Dead forms sat in pews, and the attackers were gone, banished through the disappearing portals that had brought them here, or disintegrated to dancing motes of dust.

The Kid's hand wrapped around the handle of the dagger, and it was hot in his grip.

He was back in the present, and the dead forms were slowing, stopping, and kneeling in front of him.

Overwhelmed for a moment, he collapsed to his knees, breathing heavily like he'd just run the most frantic marathon he'd ever run.

The Kid looked at the weapon in his hand. It was a simple design, common almost, but the blade was a bone white metal with a slightly serrated edge, and the handle wrapped in blood-red, soft, leather.

Looking at the bowing corpses, he saw them begin to discorporate and fade from existence. Long dead remains appeared on the floor around the room. Pews became broken and burnt, and the few remaining items that had decorated the walls fell into ruin, returning to the state they'd been within the vision, if you added many centuries of time to them.

"What the hell is going on," the Kid muttered, running his fingers through his hair.

Yeah, okay, the dagger said in his head, *you aren't the best choice, and aren't really worthy, but I guess it's better than waiting another six-thousand years for someone else.*

The chamber rumbled, and a fist-sized stone fell from the ceiling a few meters from the Kid. Another clattered on a broken pew across the room. A half dozen more, in various parts of the room, followed suit.

You might, the voice said, *want to remove yourself from the premises immediately.*

The trail of oil fed fires doused as sand and earth drifted across them from the rapidly decaying ceiling. The light went out.

Another rumble, and the rain of stone intensified.

Now, the voice was whimsical, but had an edge to it, *would be better than later.*

The Kid stood, shoved his satchel behind him from where it had fallen at his side, and ran.

He ran blindly in the dark.

Not that way, the dagger advised, *that's the way you came. Remember, 'shitter's full'? Go the other way, through either of the passages to the north. Both lead outside, and away from certain death. Here, let me help.*

The interior of the building lit with a dim glow, the sight of the being within the magical weapon extending to its wielder.

The Kid spun, sliding to his knees in the dust coating the floor, stood up, and ran in the other direction.

A floor plan popped into his head, showing him that the way out was a few meters away. Just go through the open doorway, follow it out, and into the waiting holy grove.

More stones fell, the Kid dodging around them.

The Kid moved into the right-hand passage, sprinting, and felt a breeze and smelled fresh air.

Veering right, he followed the passage and the smell of freedom, and saw the dim light of dusk ahead of him. Interwoven branches blocked it and leaves where the holly and mistletoe had grown to cover the entrance over centuries of being unattended.

He ran straight into the tangle, slashing at the branches with the dagger, and pulling at them with his free hand.

Ugh, the dagger said into his mind, *this is so below me.*

"Shut up," the Kid growled.

A rumble, a cloud of dust, and a rush of air as the underground compound collapsed followed him, throwing him face first into the underbrush blocking his way.

Pushing through the vegetation, the Kid emerged into the last remnants of daylight. Stumbling forward, he collapsed to the ground and looked around, still holding the dagger.

The grove was a natural, rough semicircle of rock and bushes. Small protrusions of stone lined the natural amphitheater in semi-straight rows.

It wasn't always like this, the voice in his head said, sounding nostalgic, *it had beautiful carvings along the rock face, topiaries lining the edges, and stone seats for people to sit on during sermons and gatherings.*

"Who are you?" the Kid asked with exasperation, holding the dagger up to eye level.

I am, the dagger sighed in the Kid's mind, *I don't think you could pronounce it, but it's a bit like this.*

"I may surprise you…" the Kid started to say, but was cut off as a flood of concepts bombarded him.

Dragons, flights of hundreds of huge reptilian beings, were the beginning of what the mystical artifact showed the Kid. The color of belief, and a burst of the emotion of passion and inner drive, followed it.

Edsumar'granoo-fisgobske-haistevan'zazott, was the jumbled word that would be the dagger's name.

After a few moments of waiting for his head to stop spinning and his stomach to stop turning, the Kid held his hand to his head and rubbed his eyes.

"Nope," the Kid said, "you're right. I'm not even going to try to pronounce that goobly-gook. I can call you Dragon's Dagger, and that's the best you're going to get."

How about Edsumar? That's a nickname I went by among your kind, the voice in the Kid's head said, and it felt like it nodded. *If that's ok, that'll do. And why is it so crowded in your head? It's like you have more than just you and me in here.*

"I can handle Edsumar. And to answer your question, it's a long story," the Kid stood, "and one I'd rather not go into."

Ah, Edsumar said, and the feeling of understanding was in the words, *I see. Very well, that'll do.*

"Just don't add pig after 'That'll do', and we'll be okay."

You do come from an odd place, Edsumar said.

"Stay out of there," the Kid said and mentally clamped down.

Oh ho, Edsumar sounded pleased, *you do have some strength to you. Good, that'll make this easier. I think we need to go north towards the home of the dragons.*

"Oh really, do you now?" the Kid said aloud, "And why would I do that?"

Because you have nowhere better to go? Edsumar said. *And I have a sense of the world. You seek adventure, right? To live life to the fullest and all that stuff? Well, I can point you in the right direction.*

"Yeah, okay," the Kid turned in the direction he thought the dagger meant, "I guess I can do that. It might be a long walk, but we'll get there."

No need, Edsumar sounded smug in the Kid's head, *I have summoned a ride for us.*

"You have Uber here?" the Kid asked, surprised.

What is an Uber? the dagger asked, a gust of wind stirring up a cloud of dust.

The Kid's next words were cut off as a shape blocked out the light of the setting sun.

A gigantic form, winged with a long neck, settled onto the ridge above the Kid. Looking up with wide eyes, the Kid stumbled backwards and fell on his ass.

"Really?" he squeaked. "A mother chuzzing dragon?"

Chapter 11

Hope's Hollow lay shrouded in a tint of orange clouds for more than a day when the Kid sauntered into it. Trinity, the human nickname of the dragon who'd flown him from the temple ruins, had dropped him off within a two-hour walk from the village.

The dragon had been a fascinating conversationalist, and apparently one of the last remaining of her kind out of the score of dragons to have survived the Downfall. The creatures were feared and despised by what were called the civilized races—humans, rokairn, aeifain, dasism, and others—and had withdrawn to the Wandering Hills many millennia ago after the Wizard Wars.

They'd built an idyllic society away from people, in what others had dubbed the wild lands. In the sprawling ridges of the mountains, they'd called to creatures to come and settle in their territory. Herds of deer and goats, and caravans of humans had answered the call. The people had settled into fertile valleys, raised herds of domesticated cattle, and harvested plentiful crops.

The dragons and people lived in a symbiotic relationship, the former providing protection and the latter providing a constant source of food with their livestock.

Trinity had talked with the Kid, exchanging stories of times gone, passing on the oral history of dragons on the continent of Teurone in this world called

Aertheia to this one lone human who was a stranger to the land.

Edsumar had remained quiet most of the time, though apparently it could speak freely into the mind of its wielder and any dragon within a certain distance.

The Kid learned from Trinity that Edsumar had been a leader of their kind, and was also the dragon slain in the battle the Kid had seen in his vision in the catacombs. The dragon's essence transferred, along with the essence of the five reptilian priests, into the dagger in the ritual. The same dagger that the Kid now carried at his hip—wrapped in a rough wooden sheath he'd whittled on the trip—across from the wavy, stolen blade of Jakdin.

The orange cloud cover worried the Kid, and he walked to the village, keeping one eye on the sky and one on the trail. The winds blew warm from the west, and the birds and insects had fallen almost completely silent, only making noise when disturbed by the Kid's passing.

Hope's Hollow lay at the eastern end of a passage through the Wandering Hills. It was a cluster of hovels and huts, mostly of woven branches and mud-made clay bricks. The ground, partially covered with leaves shed by an early cold snap, showed a path winding its way through the fallen vegetation towards the settlement.

The air held that crisp feel of autumn, and the gentle scent of decaying life as the world inevitably turned towards the dying season. The scents blended with an odd partner, a tinge of rusting iron, a metallic coppery scent that reminded the Kid of blood in your mouth after biting your tongue. He glanced up at the clouds again, watching them slide and shift against one another for a few moments.

Two men and a short woman stepped away from a small, partially concealed, lean-to at the edge of the village, armed with scythes and pitchforks.

"What do you want?" A man with steel-colored hair held a pitchfork across his body and blocked the path.

"Richeal," the woman moved up next to the man, "don't be rude, he's barely more than a child."

The Kid eyed the three, sizing them up.

The man who'd spoken was broad and thick, not from overeating, but from working, and carried himself with a threatening bravado. The Kid had dealt with men like this his whole other life.

The short woman was middle-aged, but still had smooth skin even though her hair, which she'd pulled up into a bun on her head, showed thick streaks of white.

The third man was drawn and thin, flesh hanging off his jaws, with an expression that matched it.

Most men could be sorted into one of three groups, from what the Kid had seen in nearly eighty years of living in what had often been described as a man's world. The first type was bold and often bullies. The second type were meek and often walked on. The third was a balance between the two, but almost always started as one type or the other, and changed through learning and experience.

The man named Richeal seemed to be the third type, but the Kid couldn't yet pick out if he'd started out as a bully or meek. Time would show everyone's roots and true colors, eventually.

"Well, I think we've had enough strangers here recently," the other man, who was definitely the meek type, whined and leaned around Richeal to look at the newcomer, "and it doesn't bode well. The priestess was one thing, but the barbarian yesterday, and now this one, both arriving with the blood-tainted clouds hanging above us? It bodes ill, mark my words."

"Oh Shena," the woman said scornfully, turning to roll her eyes at the man, "go grow some tea leaves and find some bones in the pig pen and become a soothsayer if you want us to listen to your constant dire warnings, will you?"

She turned back to the Kid.

"I'm Eloise," the woman smiled, and gestured to each of the men in turn, "this is Shena and Richeal, and don't pay them much mind. They've been around long enough to be wary of anything and everything, but I have more sense than they do. Come on, I'll escort you in."

The woman leaned on her scythe and held her arm out for the Kid to take. He did, and they walked into the village, arm in arm.

She talked as they went, telling the Kid about what the place had been like when the first twenty people had settled here, about five years ago. Eloise had been here about five months.

She mentioned how people had come and gone—some dying, others just leaving—and how it wasn't uncommon for a half-dozen people to leave one day without warning and a wagon train to pull in the next week with twenty new people to settle. Before she had arrived, about four-hundred people lived here, and now about two hundred and fifty, but more than half of them had shown up after she had taken up residence.

The plague had taken a lot of people from them, but more were already showing up. Like the new priestess, Esperanza, that Shena had mentioned, or the Barbarian, Torrents, who'd brought with him a lost son of the village, Axle.

The Kid listened without interest when the woman began, but then thought about the law of coincidences, and how Edsumar had mentioned something about adventure in this direction. The dagger had been suspiciously quiet over the past few days, and the Kid was unsure if it was just sleeping or what was going on. Who could know the mind of a powerful dragon stuck inside a knife, anyway?

In less than ten minutes–they'd walked slowly to allow Eloise to talk–the two arrived in the village. People went about mundane tasks, but each looked at Eloise and the newcomer with mistrustful looks.

A man herded a flock of geese down the muddy road; the butcher hung sides of swine up; the baker stood next to the blacksmith—each in the apron of their profession—wiping his flour covered hands on his stained apron while discussing some topic or another with the burly, bearded man; and a dozen other common activities of small settlements everywhere were happening under the strange sky.

In the center of the cluster of buildings was a well, about two meters across, with people clustered there to trade goods and gossip.

A dark-haired woman, assisted by a smiling, craggy-faced woman, bent over a group of children, checking them over, looking into their eyes, and inspecting their hands and arms.

An enormous man, who stood almost thirty centimeters taller than everyone around him, followed by a smaller blonde man, carried two empty barrels into the crowd and set them down. The smaller man began dickering over the price of the barrels with a third man.

It was all very normal, which was odd, considering that this world wasn't very normal.

Eloise introduced the Kid around, and he earned even more apprehensive looks when he introduced himself as 'the Kid'.

Eloise told the Kid to pick an empty hut to make his own, and was kind enough to recommend one at the edge of the settlement that wasn't in too much disarray.

After meeting a few more people, purchasing a loaf of bread, bartering for a rasher of bacon with a tin box, and filling his canteen at the well, the Kid headed to the recommended dwelling.

Thunder crackled and fell into a slow rumble as the Kid pushed open the door and looked inside. It was a one-room hovel with a fire pit in one corner, a shelf over it, and a broken crate beside it. A moth-eaten blanket and a chair with three legs were the only other things in the place. The ceiling showed the eerie sky through a handful of holes that needed to be thatched.

"Well," the Kid said to the empty room, "I've slept in worse, and at least I'll have a roof, sort of, above my head tonight."

He gathered some kindling and firewood from the nearby woods, went in, and closed the door behind him. Settling onto the three-legged chair, leaning it against a wall so it would stand, he ate some of what he'd bought and a bit of cheese he had in his bag that had been wrapped in cloth. He washed it down with his water and followed that with a swig of whiskey from the flask he kept in his boot.

Pulling out his bedroll, and using his satchel as a pillow, he settled in for a nap. It took him longer than normal to doze off, his mind working at a problem that it couldn't quite figure out if it was real or just paranoia. Something was not quite kosher.

He slept.

The Kid woke, and the room was dark, except for the odd orange light emanating from the clouds. The thunder rolled, an almost constant low rumble overhead. Flashes of green heat lightning accompanied the noise.

The Kid was used to staying up most of the night, going to sleep a few hours before dawn, and then waking up just before noon.

So was Jen, said Edsumar in the Kid's head.

"So now you're around?" the Kid scoffed and shook his head.

Edsumar didn't answer.

The Kid went about his routine, scrubbing at his pits and bits with a wet cloth, then doing a quick wipe of the rest of him, one part at a time, undressing and dressing as he cleaned up.

He crept into the night, having decided to look around once everyone was asleep. People asked fewer questions about why you were in their house if they weren't awake. And you could find a lot more answers, a lot quicker, that way.

After checking a dozen huts, he was pretty confident there wasn't much here worth knowing, let alone stealing.

He stood in the shadows, watching the butcher creep back to his own house from the blacksmith's—a late-night, secret rendezvous, no doubt—and snickered as he thought about what the two men's wives would think.

A sudden squeak from the baker made the Kid turn back to look in that direction.

In the glow of orange clouds above, the Kid saw Eloise standing over the baker, who'd fallen to knees and then backwards to the ground, with the scythe buried in his chest.

She chanted quietly and sprinkled crushed herbs on the man. A moment later, she pulled a stoppered beaker from a pouch, and poured a viscous liquid into the throat of the dead man.

A green orb of lightning shot from the clouds above and slammed into the man's body. The corpse on the ground lurched and shuddered, then sat up.

Eloise pulled the scythe from the chest of her new minion; the Kid could see the curved blade of the reaping tool drinking in the blood that coated it.

"Rise," Eloise intoned in a smoky voice, "rise, my child, and join your brethren."

The shadows in the tree line behind the woman shifted, then moved, as dozens of undead creatures lurched, shambled, scrambled, bounced, and crept forward.

"Oh, chuz," the Kid muttered.

Eloise raised her eyes to look at him and smiled.

Chapter 12

Eloise's hair was no longer streaked with white, or in a bun on her head. It was bright red and flared around her face and shoulders. The woman's clothing was no longer drab colors in a simple village style. Instead, it was a midnight blue robe with runes of silver thread decorating the cuffs and hem.

She took a step towards the Kid.

The Kid had dealt with powerful people—in both worlds—more times than he could count. He'd dealt with store managers, bikers, CEOs, military leaders, teenage high school students, politicians, and others in the old world. He'd dealt with assassins, murderers, thieves, angry fishwives, irate city guards, and drunken perverts in this world. Actually, that second group could have been in either world. But he'd never dealt with a necromancer backed by a hungry horde of magically animated and loyal corpses.

The Kid stumbled backwards, falling to his ass, and then crab-crawled backwards until he hit a wall. His eyes darted from her to the undead creatures moving forward into the village, and soon she was lost to his sight.

He crab-walked up the wall until he was standing. The whole time he was doing 'hfrah-frahl-hraf' sound, like when someone takes too large of a bite of steaming hot food, and was trying to cool it while it was still in their mouth. In truth, he was trying to work up the breath to scream.

That task was taken from him when the creatures behind the woman fanned out and began rushing into hovels.

At first, it just a couple surprised yells, but in less than a minute, it had become a chorus of screams and panicked shouting from dozens of different huts. Villagers poured out of their shacks and into the mud road that meandered through the center of the town. Screams were cut off in mid-breath as people were taken down in the street under the blood tint emanating from the clouds.

"By Senaria's Honor," boomed a deep shout, and a bare-chested warrior with a sword almost as long as he was tall burst from a rickety door. The rotting creatures were thrown back by twos and threes with each sweep of the man's mighty blade.

Torrence had woken to the slight sound of the hut's door opening and the shuffle of feet across the dirt floor. He'd turned to his side, his hand dropping to his sword's pommel—which had lain beside his pallet—lofted the weapon, rolled to the floor, swung his sword, disemboweled the creature.

Leaping to his feet, he ran out the door. His momentum had carried him into two more of the creatures, and they'd flown backwards when he ran through them.

Torrence had always loved good action flicks since he was a boy. Anything with Bruce Willis, Tom Cruise, or Dwayne Johnson was sure to be a favorite of his. He loved how they moved from one foe to the other without ever raising a sweat. It reminded him of his years as a high school quarterback when he'd run a sneak, weaving and spinning around the other team until he came out of the clump of boys and could sprint down the field.

But it wasn't like that in an actual fight. You got tangled in an enemy's grasp, or caught from behind, or your sweaty palms made the sword slip when you hit something.

It just wasn't the same, he thought, his bare foot sliding out from under him on a rock no bigger than a peach pit.

He caught himself before he fell, regaining his footing, but he was sure he now bled from the bottom of that foot.

Axle followed behind, using the massive form of the larger man as a blocker, and stabbing out with a thin sword and a similar, but unmatched, dagger. Slinking along behind Torrents, he slashed from the safety of the big man's shadow, literally and figuratively. He believed in playing it safe, and something as big as Torrents would be a waste to not use as cover.

His rapier jabbed into an eye, his dagger slicing under an armpit to cut tendons, and he moved constantly.

From the other direction, purplish lightning crashed down in the night and struck the earth. A handful of the vile things attacking Hope's Hollow flew in all directions.

A woman stood in the clearing smoke, her grey robe hung open and flapped in the night wind, revealing a plain cotton shift underneath with a symbol of Latress atop it. Her fists were balled at her sides, her face twisted, her jaw clenched with rage. Both her eyes and hands crackled and glowed with the same energy that had just obliterated the creatures in the lightning strike.

Esperanza was full of righteous fury. She'd woken to the screams of villagers in the distance, and Rose shouting from a meter away. The woman was beating some twisted form with a chair, kicking at it as it went down. The woman was also laughing between the shouts and curses.

Without thinking, Esperanza had snatched her robe, knife, and holy symbol from the peg on the wall, threw them on, and then called upon the power of Latress. A tendril of wind had snapped the thing from the floor and shot it out the door and into three others.

Esperanza stormed after it, in more ways than one.

She might be in her own personal hell, but she would not see others tortured for her sins. And she would not give up. If God wanted to test her, then she would use the tools she was given to crush this test, even if it meant using the powers of some pagan, heathen god. After all, the Bible mentioned other gods in almost two dozen different places.

A haggard woman, with a wicked smile of glee showing the few teeth left in her mouth, followed behind the priestess, kicking at the fallen creatures, or bashing them with a wooden chair leg.

Rose was committed to staying at Esperanza's side and giving whatever help she could. She'd seen this woman save the lives of more than a hundred people, die, and then rise again as a different woman. Esperanza's face even looked different, her skin a lovely almond color, her hair seemed longer, and Rose swore the priestess had been taller before her death.

When the two women's path crossed anyone in need of help, they paused to do so.

"Oh, okay," the Kid sighed, and pushed himself from the wall, drawing his stolen sword and the Dragon's Dagger in the same movement.

The Kid spun into the battle, slicing and slashing, then moving and weaving deeper into the fray. His weapons cut and bit, tearing down the undead like a well-honed machete tears through a field of weeds and saplings.

He dodged into the shadows beside a hut, crouching and waiting for one of the lumbering monstrosities to wander by so he could strike without being seen. His vision was clear, and he could see as well in the dark shadows as he could in the eerie light from above, thanks to the dagger's magics.

But the element of surprise didn't work out quite the way the Kid had hoped. Four of the rotting forms turned and looked straight at him.

"Great," he muttered, "of course the dead can see in the dark. Why wouldn't they be able to see in the dark. After all, they're dead."

The things may have been able to see him, but they weren't smart, and they bee-lined for him.

Once they were close enough, the Kid shot to his feet, his left hand holding the dagger traced a line from the first creature's groin, up its stomach and ribs. The Kid, flicking the point of the weapon upwards, pierced the bottom of the thing's chin, and slid the blade into its brain.

The sword in his right hand thrust forward, turning sideways so the flat of the blade was parallel to the ground. When it hit a second creature's chest, the tip slid along a rib and moved between it and the next rib, and slipped into the thing's heart.

Both creatures crumpled to the ground. And the next two followed just as quickly.

The Kid stepped from the shadows into the street and looked around for the next opponent.

Torrence—surrounded by a mound of writhing, broken undead forms—shouted an unintelligible war cry and leaped over the bodies, running towards the pale line of figures in the trees that stood watching.

"Torrents!" Axle shouted. "don't go there, not yet, let's regroup first!"

The barbarian slowed, looked over his shoulder at his friend, back towards the dozens of waiting things, and then stopped.

Esperanza looked around. The village was a charnel field. Bodies of undead lay heaped among the newly dead corpses of the villagers.

Rose raised a hand and waved the few remaining villagers still alive to come to her, nodded at Torrence, and then at the Kid.

The clouds overhead growled again, causing all eyes to raise to the heavens. They split to reveal hundreds of green globes of energy spinning in orbit around a deep red, pulsing core.

A woman's voice began chanting, and the people who remained alive looked towards the sound. Eloise stood atop the largest building in the village, the blacksmith's stable and shed, her arms raised as she called upon the elements and gods to do her will.

The sickly verdant balls shot downward, each one striking and then sinking into a motionless corpse. Villagers, and some of her own minions that had been struck down.

Bodies twitched. As the survivors looked on in horror, they saw bone knit, organs drawn back into torsos, muscles come together, and skin draw back into puckered scars by some invisible force.

Then the dead began to rise. The butcher staggered into the village center, followed by the steel-haired Richeal. Shena pushed past Bert and Frebel, while leaning on the blacksmith.

The creatures struck down in the battle also rose, their recently gained wounds now just furrowed, greying flesh.

"Run!" came the shout from Axle, and he did as he commanded.

Grabbing Torrence's arm as he moved past him, he pulled the large man behind him.

Torrence resisted for a moment, before common sense overcame battle lust, and he ran as well.

The Kid was already paralleling the two paths, not wanting to be close enough to get trapped in an ambush, but not wanting to lose sight of them in a part of the country he didn't know.

Esperanza called upon the power of her goddess, but stopped when she realized Rose was tugging on her arm.

"We can't save them all, priestess," Rose said, her eyes wide and scared, "they're already dead."

She waved a hand at the hundreds of bodies staggering to their numb feet. Then jabbed a finger towards the dozen or so remaining people who were actually alive, and not just rictus puppets of dead flesh.

"But," Rose continued, still pulling on Esperanza, "we might save a few. We need to go now. We've done all we can here."

Esperanza let out her breath, seeming to deflate in defeat, and all the energy went out of her body. The light went from her eyes and hands, and she was just a woman again.

She nodded and let Rose pull her after the others, into the dark night as the orange clouds faded to a dull grey above them.

Chapter 13

"Why would any of us listen to you?" Esperanza jabbed a finger repeatedly into Torrence's chest.

Rose tried to pull the priestess away by her shoulder.

"And you," Esperanza shrugged off Rose's hand and spun to face her, "you had us all run into the night, save the few, chuz the many. We might've been able to save more."

"Pfft," the Kid said, not even looking up from where he leaned against a tree and cleaned his nails, "girl, you would've just died with the rest of them, and probably got your friend and the remaining villagers turned into one of those things to boot."

Esperanza's face was already red, but now she was sputtering.

"Stop being such a child," the Kid said, "and face the facts; your friend is right; you have a death wish or are trying to prove something; the big guy was just doing what comes natural to him; and if we didn't get away when we did, we'd all be dead, or worse."

"Who the hell are you?" Torrence turned towards the Kid, and stood shoulder to shoulder with Esperanza, "and what the hell gives you the right to talk that way to a grown woman, punk?"

"I can fight my own battles," Esperanza spat the words at Torrence, "thank you very much. I don't need some bone head, muscle bound, creep trying to charge in and save me. Mind your own damned business, okay?"

"No," Torrence turned back to the priestess, and had to look down to look her in the eye, "as far as I can tell, this is my business. This is everyone who's here business. And I'd appreciate if you didn't just assume that I'm a pemtie because I'm big!"

"I don't assume you're a pemtie because you're big," Esperanza was jabbing him in the chest again, "I assume it because your pemtie."

"Oh," Torrence threw up his hands, mocking her and causing her to flinch back, "good come back, your mom write that for you?"

"Moms have been around," the Kid muttered, "and they know some pretty damned good come backs."

The two spun to face the Kid again.

"Did you just say," Torrence growled and took a step towards the Kid, "that my mom got around?"

"Okay, already!" Axle stepped between the big guy and the Kid, putting a hand on the barbarian's chest to halt him. Axle slid almost a meter before the man stopped. "Let's not do the job that the necromancer failed to do. Everyone just take a step back and a deep breath."

"We did a good thing," Rose said, her hands on her hips, glaring at Esperanza.

Rose hadn't ever seen the priestess like this before. As fear had taken the place of kindness, now anger had taken the place of fear.

Last night, they'd run from the village, gathering what people they could. Fourteen people were with them now, including herself, Axle, and the three that kept on arguing.

Axle had stepped into the role of a natural leader, with Rose mothering and herding the others along. The other dozen people were like lost sheep between the trauma of last night, and just who they normally were. Rose comforted and guided, Axle organized and gave out tasks.

The group had spent the night clustered together under an outcropping of rock in the foothills to the west. The orange clouds had dissipated, and the storm that had waited above, broke.

They'd returned to Hope's Hollow about noon the following day. The village had been deserted. No trace of the people or creatures from last night remained, other than remnants of the battle on the muddy road or inside huts.

After deciding they wouldn't stay here any longer, the group had gathered what little belongings they could take with them. Nothing had been looted. Apparently, Eloise, the necromancer, only took her things, and a walking dead army didn't need supplies.

A small group of new additions stood to one side, under the boughs of a large tree, and huddled in their cloaks, clutching their belongings.

Torrence turned his back to everyone, throwing a dagger into a stump. Esperanza was on the opposite side of the group, muttering angrily in a rapid language that the others didn't recognize.

"Where do we go from here, Rose?" Axle asked quietly.

The two had stepped away from the various clumps of people without planning it, and Axle had taken that moment to speak to the only other person with a level head.

"I honestly don't have a clue, Axle," Rose said, smiling up at the man, though the rest of her face showed unease.

She looked strained and tired. But they all did.

"It's gonna be okay," Axle said as he put a hand on her shoulder and rubbed it.

Rose leaned into it a little, glad for some comfort and human contact.

"I have an idea," the Kid said, making both Axle and Rose jump.

Neither had seen him there, or heard him come up.

"Where?" Axle said and realized his voice sounded angry.

"Am I interrupting?" The Kid raised his eyebrows and looked back and forth between the two with a small smile.

Axle adjusted his tone and asked, "Where do you think we can go? It has to be close enough that we can take all these people, walking, and dragging wagons and wheelbarrows. And it has to be somewhere that'll take in people who have nothing to offer except themselves. That means extra mouths to feed until they get on their feet again. And winter'll be here soon, there's not time for them to grow crops, or even stockpile enough wood to last the snows."

The Kid nodded.

"Yeah," the Kid said casually, "I know all that. I've been around long enough to know how the world works."

"So," Rose said coaxingly, and put a hand on the Kid's forearm, "where is this place?"

"I'll tell you," the Kid said, looking down at the hand on his arm, "but you're going to think I'm crazy."

"Uh huh," Axle laughed, "Kid, I think we're all little crazy right now. Just tell us and let us decide if it's crazy."

"Okay," the Kid stepped away from the two, Rose's hand falling away.

He began pacing.

"On my way here, I met a very nice…" the Kid hesitated, his lips slipping between a smirk and a grimace, "lady on the trip. Her name is Trinity. She's very old, but doesn't act it, and very nice. She told me about a place where lots of people once lived. They're gone now. I think that happened in the Downfall."

"It sounds perfect," Rose said. "Is it far away?"

"Hold on," Axle said with suspicion and amusement in his voice, "I think there's a big 'but' coming soon. Go on, Kid, finish your story."

"Well," the Kid went on, plucking a leaf from the tree above him and tearing into small pieces, "I think they'll have left behind a lot of supplies, dry goods, maybe even grain and seeds. There's a possibility that their herds still roam the area, though they've indubitably all gone wild by now. And the place is sheltered and protected. I think it'd be a good fit."

"Uh huh," Axle said, putting a hand on Rose's arm to stall her questions, "and where is it?"

"It's called Dargaon's Hole…" the Kid began.

"And there it is!" Axle threw his hands into the air, laughing.

"What?" Rose asked, reaching for the man. "What's wrong with this place?"

"It's the ancestral home where dragons lived," Axle explained, still laughing, "and where they kept people as cattle for food."

"I don't think that matters anymore," Rose said. "It's not like there are any more dragons."

"Well," the Kid drew the word out.

Both stopped and looked at him.

The Kid now had an entire branch of leaves he was plucking at.

"Go on," Axle said, folding his arms across his chest.

"First," the Kid held up one finger, smiling, "they never ate people. The people raised livestock for them to eat. And in trade, the dragons gave them shelter and protection."

"Uh huh," Axle grunted, "what else?"

"And there might be a dragon left," the Kid's voice slowed and dropped until it was a mumble by the end of the sentence.

"But she's very nice," the Kid said, louder and emphatically, resembling an actual child trying to convince their parents to let him do something they didn't approve of, "and she didn't eat me, so she's unlikely to eat you guys, and you guys could rebuild their thing back to how it was. You know, work together."

Axle was now laughing hard, holding his sides, and sliding to his knees onto the wet grass.

Rose had seen people who needed a release after a huge stressful or traumatic event. Some cried, others laughed. Axle, apparently, was a laugher. She put a hand on his shoulder.

"Well," the Kid said, now with his arms folded across his chest, "are you guys going to go?"

"Sure." Axle patted Rose's hand as he wiped tears from his eyes. "Why not? I mean, we're all just as likely to die out here from exposure or bandits or slavers or mutant bunnies. So, why not?"

"Hold on," Rose said, looking at the Kid with slitted eyes, "what do you mean, 'you guys'? Aren't you coming also?"

"Um, no." the Kid said simply.

"And why not?" Axle asked, standing and wiping at the mud on his knees.

"I'm going after the necromancer." The Kid held up his hand to stop them before they could say anything. "I showed up here for a reason, and I didn't know what that was. Now, I'm pretty sure I know. I'm going after the necromancer."

"Okay Kid," Axle said, "you do what you need to do, it's your funeral."

"How do we get there?" Rose asked.

"Um," the Kid's brow furrowed.

You'll draw them a map, Edsumar said in the Kid's head. *I know the way. And I'll let Trinity know they're coming. But you might not want to tell them that part.*

"I'll draw you a map," the Kid smiled and looked around for a dry spot to do just that.

"How're we going to convince the others to go?" Rose asked Axle.

"Just tell them," the Kid shouted over his shoulder, "Come with me, if you want to live."

They watched the Kid walk away laughing.

"See?" Axle said to Rose, "we're all a little crazy here."

They turned towards the groups of frightened people to give them the news, but stopped when they saw Torrence and the priestess standing next to each other in a heated discussion.

"Uh oh," Rose said, "looks like we forgot the leave the kids with a babysitter, and they're fighting again."

Axle chuckled, and they headed for the pair.

Torrence and Esperanza looked up when they approached, both chagrinned.

"We have a place to go," Axle said. "The Kid, of all people, knows a place and it sounds pretty good. So, come with us if you want to live."

Both Torrence and Esperanza appeared startled at Axle's words.

"You two alright?" Rose asked, putting a hand on Esperanza's arm.

"Yeah," the priestess said, fingering her sheathed blade, "but I'm afraid we won't be going with you."

"We're going after that god-damned undead army," Torrence said.

Rose and Axle exchanged amused looks.

"Language," Esperanza crossed her arms, an accent creeping into her voice, "and don't take the Lord's name in vain."

Torrence's head snapped to look at her, a surprised look on his face.

She looked away, not wanting to start another fight.

"Looks like you won't be alone," Axle said. "The Kid's going that way too. Guess you can all go together."

Esperanza looked dismayed as she turned to the man, and Torrence snapped his head back to Axle, Esperanza's comment forgotten.

"No," the barbarian and priestess said together.

Chapter 14

The Black Wood gained its name for three different reasons. The first was the shade of the trees, many of them walnut trees that had a naturally dark brown bark, but others were maple trees with a fungal growth, causing their trunks to appear almost black. This, in addition to how close and thick they grew to one another, caused most of the forest to be in constant shade.

The second reason was because this was where armies had clashed. Most recently in the Downfall, where demon armies met dragon armies. Previously, it had been mages battling priests, and before that, it was raised by wizards as a barricade from others finding the Nine Towers of Magic.

The third reason was the most recent addition to the myths, legends, and stories; that it was haunted by remnants of dark magics, the spirits of people and demons alike, and the reflections of magic from the Nine Towers to the east, now that it was uninhabited.

The three traveled eastward, following the trail of destruction and death from the necromancer's army. Wildlife had fled with the approach of the dead, leaving the forest eerily silent. Most movement was from the wind, and the occasional insect.

On the first day, they found a herd of deer laying in scattered pieces, disemboweled. Whatever had attacked them ate what they wanted and moved on. Three deer remained, but were no longer natural.

Instead, standing on tottering legs, with sheaves of flesh torn away, leaving coagulated blood surrounding bare bone on their sides and flanks.

They stood over the remains of the herd, tearing at the flesh of their once protective circle of family. Hearing Torrence, Esperanza, and the Kid approaching, they raised their twisted muzzles, bared their deformed teeth, and hissed.

One charged at the group, only to be taken down by Torrence's arrow, slicing through its eye and into its brain just meters before it reached the trio. The three agreed they couldn't leave the remaining two here in their condition, so they killed the mutant deer.

None of the three slept well that night. When they woke the next morning, rolling out of their blankets and packing their gear, they heard an odd noise from one of the animal corpses fifty meters away.

Upon approaching the thing, it burst open with a tearing noise and a swarm of insects rose into the morning sky and circled, looking for its next meal. It settled on another deer, only to have the dead animal split in half and fist-sized, beetle-like creatures lurch out and attack the flying insects in a frenzy.

"Khelikian," Esperanza muttered, "Lord of the flies and Emperor of insects. This is his domain now, and we should take our leave."

They set up a watch, with Torrence staying awake for the first handful of hours before midnight. He woke the Kid for the second watch, and the Kid woke Esperanza a few hours before dawn.

Two more days brought real animals back into the area. They heard squirrels and chipmunks scurry across dried leaves, or above in the tree branches. They saw racoons and possum moving through the underbrush, and even spotted a black bear clawing at a fallen tree, tearing away the bark to get to the grubs and bugs beneath.

The weather continued to be wet for those first few days, but as the temperature dropped, the rain dissipated, though the sky remained grey, and the clouds heavy.

It was hard to get their bearings in that weather, and with none of them being a woodsman, they did the best they could by finding moss-covered trees to help orient where north was.

When the Kid asked the barbarian why he wasn't better at this sort of thing, he answered he wasn't what he once was, and predominately knew the northern tundra and grasslands of the Frozen Desert.

On the fifth day, as they took a break around noon, sitting beside a stream to fill their canteens and waterskins, Esperanza spoke.

"I think we're being followed," the priestess said, "I haven't seen anything, but I feel something."

"Is your Spidey-sense tingling?" the Kid laughed, "Or your priestess-senses? Some disturbance in the dark side?"

"What did you just say?" Esperanza turned towards the Kid, reaching for him.

"Hush," Torrence hissed.

They twisted to look at him.

The big man crouched and crept forward on the balls of his feet, barely making a sound.

Esperanza looked back to the Kid to see him disappearing up a tree, only his calves and boots still visible as he climbed higher.

The priestess turned away to see a low, dark form darting between the trees.

Torrence skulked towards it, his left hand held in front of him, and his sword in the defensive stance he often used. The weapon was parallel to the ground, just above the height of the man's head, his elbow bent, the tip pointed in the direction the barbarian moved.

Esperanza fumbled with her holy symbol, and words of prayer to Latress filled her mind. She stopped, just as she was about to call upon the power she had access to, and forcibly dropped the medallion around her neck. Standing up straight, she thrust her hands to her sides, one gripping her knife, and the other clenched into a fist.

The Kid found a vantage point in the thick leaves above the forest floor. He watched Esperanza fidget and wondered why the woman fought with the powers she was given. Watching his companions, the Kid suspected that the three of them might have more in common than they knew.

Torrence moved forward slowly. The warrior's head pivoted, watching for movement in the trees.

"Watch out!" the Kid yelled, sitting up and straddling the branch, drawing his dagger.

Two forms slid from the shadows and leaped at Torrence.

The Kid pulled his arm back and let the weapon fly. Its course wobbled, then straightened itself, curving to hit its target.

Torrence heard the warning, but didn't look up. In the zone, his mind quieted as his senses took over. He could smell the ozone of the supernatural, mixing with the fetid aroma of rotting leaves, as his grandfather had taught him on the plains when he was just a child.

The warrior's ears picked up every sound; from the Kid above him, to Esperanza shuffling behind him, to the barely audible padding of a predator within the tree line. His eyes caught movement, his muscles loose but ready to tighten, to act in a heartbeat.

All this passed without a thought, and when the creature launched itself at Torrence, his sword moved on its own, slicing towards the leaping beast.

The thing went down; the sword passing above it. A dagger sunk into its skull where it met the neck; the beast collapsed to the ground and slid along the wet leaves until its nose reached the barbarian's feet.

The jaws moved, trying to snap at its prey, even though the body couldn't respond.

Torrence flipped his sword downward, grabbed the pommel in both hands, and thrust it into the beast's heart.

Baying sounded to the barbarian's right. In the distance, to his left, an answering cry rose. A third, fourth, and fifth joined the chorus until the only sound the three heard was the song of predators calling to their pack.

A silhouette stepped from behind a tree in the distance. Inhumanly thin and taller than a man, it drew in the dappled sunlight around it and devoured it by merely standing near it.

It pointed at Torrence.

A form tackled the barbarian from the right, knocking him to the ground, his sword flying into the underbrush. Teeth snapped at his face, huge paws pinning the man to the earth.

He rolled, throwing the beast atop him to one side.

It skidded to a halt three paces away, turning back towards Torrence. It resembled a wolf, in that it was a canine with fur, but that's where the similarities ended.

It was as long as a wolf but lower to the ground, with shorter legs, and its coat wiry and coarse, as dark as the fungus-infected tree bark around them. Its snout was stubby and thick, and its long tail bristled with fur and thin spikes.

The thief dropped from above, blade piercing the skull of the animal, landing on its back. A cracking sound filled the area as the animal's back broke.

The Kid looked up and winked.

"I guess it wasn't that dog's day, was it?" the Kid smirked.

"There's more coming," Torrence scrambled to recover his sword.

"You think?" Esperanza said. "We need to get away from here!"

"They'll run us down," Torrence said. "they might not be fast, but they know how to track, and they'll move through the underbrush quicker and easier than we will."

"Into the trees, then," the Kid pulled his white-bladed dagger from the body of the first creature and moved to climb another tree.

"They'll just wait us out," Torrence shook his head, "we'll have to come down sometime, and they'll be right here."

"They'll get tired and look for easier prey," the Kid pulled himself up to the first branch and held a hand towards Esperanza, "and then we can be on our way."

"I don't think so," Torrence shook his head again, and scanned the trees, "there's something else with them. Something not natural."

"You felt that, too?" Esperanza asked.

The Kid closed his eyes and opened his mind to others, as he'd done countless times when tracking a mark in the city. His own magical abilities allowed him to find others; it was like having another set of eyes and ears, but different. Something cold and heavy washed across his mind, and a pinprick of pain shot through his skull.

"Yeah," the Kid drawled and dropped back to the ground, "he's right. This thing is dangerous, and different, and, I think the only way I can describe it is, evil."

I could have told you that, Edsumar said into the Kid's head.

"So," the Kid bent over to pick up Esperanza's pack, and handed it to her, "I guess we do a tactical retreat then."

Chapter 15

The three ran, moving in the only direction that was away from the howling creatures. Forms darted along beside them, passing them and then stopping to watch them go by. Yips and growls were the pack communicating with one another, or distracting their quarry, as the chase went on.

Torrence sheathed his sword and held his bow in his left hand. He clutched his right arm across his chest, and blood welled from a bite mark on his bicep. He stumbled, shook his head, and wiped sweat from his eyes.

Esperanza ran, holding and lifting the hem of her robes. She panted from the exertion, but kept up. She looked at Torrence; seeing the wound, she noted it should be bleeding more. The skin around the entry points had puckered and was a bright scarlet. These things, pursuing them, must have some sort of bacteria in their mouths, similar to the Komodo dragons back home.

The Kid fell back, seeing Esperanza struggling to keep up, and Torrence hurt worse than he let on. He knew they were being herded; he'd done the same thing in the alleys of Durgan's Keep with his own sort of prey. They wouldn't last like this. One of the others would collapse sooner or later.

I could abandon them, he thought, then sighed. *No, I need them if I'm going to face off against a necromancer with an army of hundreds of undead.*

What the hell am I thinking? Facing off against a necromancer? Someone who could actually create and control the living dead? This wasn't even some sci-fi thing where people had contracted a viral infection that did messed up things to them. This was someone who dictated their every action, like some sort of giant computer game where you could direct armies with the click of a mouse. It's insanity to go up against something like that.

The Kid waited to see if Edsumar would offer some input on this one, but the magical dagger was silent.

The Kid needed a plan.

The priestess is useless unless backed into a corner, and she lost her bidj. Only then did she do anything that was helpful, he thought. *And the big guy would be face planting into the dirt sooner, rather than later.*

Okay, the Kid thought, *first things first. Get out of this mess, then deal with the impossible army.*

That means finding a place they could hide, or a place these things couldn't get to. Or cleverly killing them all in one fell swoop of impossible luck. Option two was the best, but I have no idea where to find such a place.

They'd been running for almost fifteen minutes. The trees thinned significantly, and the ground became hilly and rocky when the barbarian went down.

Esperanza ran about another ten steps before realizing it, slowing and turning back, tripping over her feet and tumbling onto the grass. She panted heavily, holding the stitch in her side as she crawled towards the man.

The forms had been pacing them for a while now, not bothering to hide from them or herd them in any direction. It had turned into a waiting game.

The Kid jogged up to the two and stood over them, his lips in a tight line, looking around to see if their position, or anything close by, was defendable at all. The answer was no to both.

The Kid sighed, drew out his sword, and loosely held the dagger in his other hand.

Esperanza rolled Torrence onto his back.

His breath came in wheezing gasps, and his eyes rolled back. He was no longer sweating, but his face was red and splotchy, and the wound in his arm had a deep purple tint to it.

"Boy, oh boy," cackled a voice, "you folks are in a bidj-ton of hurt, aren't ya?"

The Kid and Esperanza looked up, startled.

A small, thin man was sitting cross-legged on an outcropping of rock that jutted from the earth.

He wore a blend of furs and tattered cloth wrapped around his body, and his thin, wispy beard contrasted with his bald pate. He smiled, waving with one hand, and clutching a staff longer than he was tall in the other. Living vines wrapped around the wooden walking stick.

"It's that thing we felt," Esperanza gasped, "the thin man that Torrence saw!"

"No," the Kid's voice was calm, but calculating, "I don't think it is. Look at the things chasing us."

The Kid pointed to the crests of the surrounding hills. The beasts keeping pace with them crouched, hackles up, in twos and threes on top of the knolls.

"What the hell are they waiting for?" Esperanza spat, anger washing away any other emotion.

"Exactly," the Kid nodded, his eyes never leaving the small man, "I think it might be him keeping them at bay for the moment."

The man turned back and forth between the two, his head moving to look at each one as they spoke, his smile never faltering. It was like he was watching his favorite comedy routine.

"Can you help us?" the Kid gestured at the gathered beasts.

"Well," the man rubbed his white chin whiskers, "that depends how you define help. PepperGarten means PepperGarten thinks you three have bigger issues than some playful pups wanting to nibble on your toes."

One animal barked three times in quick succession, and all three-dozen leapt forward as one.

The man gave out a frustrated scream and bounded off the rock he'd been sitting on. Raising his hands, he whirled the staff above his head. Grass writhed at the edge of the small valley, and tendrils of plants burst through the soil. Vines and branches rose into the air, thickening as they grew.

The animals hit the top edge of the bramble hedge as it instantaneously grew beneath them, wrapping them in its thorny grip and tightening, expanding and blossoming.

"Doggie damn it," the withered man screeched, "PepperGarten is still talking here!"

The plant wall continued to expand and flower, though at a slower rate. Its tendril-like arms creeping around the beasts' throats and bodies, squeezing until they couldn't move. One animal let out a pained howl a moment before it exploded from the pressure of the plant's grip.

"Fine then," the man harrumphed, "if we can't have a reasonable conversation here because of these pemtie witch worgs, and their annoying hound master, then PepperGarten guesses you'll have to come for tea. Let's go."

The thin man turned and tottered towards the only opening in the wall of brambles.

He noticed the other three weren't following and turned back to them.

"Well," he put his hands on his hips, his staff jutting out in an awkward angle in front of him, "what's the matter, you don't like tea?"

"What about him?" the Kid pointed at Torrence, who lay on the ground, panting in quick breaths.

Esperanza stared, wide-eyed, between the man and the barrier that was slowly executing the animals in its grip.

"Oh, no," PepperGarten said in a mocking tone, "did someone get a wittle owie?"

The man moved forward and dropped down beside the barbarian.

"Lemme look at it," the wizened man bent over Torrence and grabbed the warrior's arm.

Torrence thrashed weakly and let out a moan of pain.

"You're hurting him." Esperanza moved next to the old man and reached to pull him away from her traveling companion.

She froze when she saw what he was doing.

The man had a handful of herbs and spat on them, then ground them into his palm, using his fist as a pestle and his hand as a mortar.

PepperGarten took a sharp, thin reed from a bag at his waist, cut a slit into the barbarian's upper arm, and then squeezed. Black ichor, mixed with thick blood and yellowish puss, oozed from the opening. The man spat into the wound and ground the herb mixture into it.

Torrence gasped and cried out, his body going rigid and lifting off the ground, though he stayed unconscious.

"Oh yeah," the old man cackled, "PepperGarten bets that hurts like hell!"

Esperanza lurched forward to pull the man away from the barbarian.

The wiry man bounced to his feet, and hopping from one foot to the other, danced back to where he'd been before.

"Ready for that tea now?" the odd little man said with a smile.

Esperanza knelt beside Torrence and inspected the injury. Small green sprouts grew from the poultice, knitting the flesh together and drawing the poison from the man.

The priestess tore a strip from the hem of her robe and lifted the man's arm to bind the healing gash.

"Don't do that," the old man said derisively. "You'll kill the cure, and you don't do that, do you?"

"How are we supposed to get him" the Kid gestured to Torrence, "to wherever we're going?"

"That's your problem," PepperGarten sniffed. "PepperGarten stopped him from dying. You don't expect PepperGarten to carry his heavy ass all the way, too, do you?"

Torrence lay on a bed of clover and grass inside the place PepperGarten called home.

It was a shelter within the root system of an enormous willow tree that leaned over a hilltop. The roots hung off the side of the hill, dug out either by man or nature, to form a hollow. Dense vines grew along the arm-thick branches that connected to the rich soil below, their leaves creating a wall to keep out the elements.

Dozens of praying mantises stood vigil on the leaves, as a handful of groundhogs nibbled at dandelions on the grass outside. A score of different breeds of birds darted in and out of the leaves above, swooping down to make a meal of fluttering moths.

A nest of squirrels, in the natural rafters of the underside of the tree, chittered in angry judgement of the guests.

A fox sat on her haunches, three kits playing at her feet with two ferrets, watching the intruders who shared her den.

PepperGarten puttered about, muttering to himself—or perhaps to the animals, it was hard to tell—dropping various berries and greens into wooden bowls. A small earthen chiminea held a ceramic teapot, heating it slowly.

"So," PepperGarten said, setting small clay cups in front of the Kid and Esperanza, "what did you pemties do to piss off a hound master so much that he brought his full contingent of witch worgs?"

Sitting on a grassy tuft, Esperanza shrugged, brushing uncomfortably at her robes to remove briars stuck there.

"I think we're just that good," the Kid smirked.

"Oh," the old man put his fists on his waist and thrust his hips forward and back, "is that so? And if that's the case, are you sure it doesn't have to do with that cranky old dagger you have on your side? How's Edsumar doing nowadays, anyway?"

The Kid jumped at the mention of the name of his magical weapon's dragon spirit.

Chapter 16

Torrence ran. The Shadow Man was right behind him, though he never seemed to move. Each time Torrence looked behind him, the Shadow was standing there watching him.

He ran through the halls of his high school, lockers flying past him as he approached the gym. His history teacher, Mr. Stevens, stepped out of a classroom. The man gasped and turned to look at Torrence rushing past him. When he looked back, the teacher was now the Shadow Man, reaching for him with long, slender fingers made of solid smoke.

Torrence tried to scream, but couldn't catch his breath.

He ran on, stumbling around the corner, and saw the gym doors in the distance, the logo of the Battling Wolfhounds, his school's mascot, emblazoned across the two doors.

Regaining his feet, he sprinted forward; the entrance seeming to recede as he tried to reach it.

He burst through the doors that had seemed so far away just a moment ago, and into the pep rally. Painted paper banners proclaimed, 'Bash the Barbarians' and other such slogans adorned the gym walls.

Torrence slowed, panting, and bent over, hands on his knees, trying to catch his breath. The crowd howled at his entrance.

He looked into the stands, and hundreds of students had heads of the creatures that had pursued him and his companions through the Black Wood.

He stumbled backwards, turning towards the door. The Shadow Man, his mouth a thin line of pearly jagged teeth, blocked his way.

The Shadow Man reached for him.

"M-my, what?" The Kid stared at PepperGarten. "Who? I don't know what you're talking about."

"That magic dagger," the man giggled, pointing, "it's been crying and whining for someone to come get it for a long time now. PepperGarten's glad it finally found some poor sucker to take it for a walk."

"Your what?" Esperanza looked at the Kid. "You have a magic dagger? Are you bidjing me?"

"Well, it doesn't do much," the Kid put a protective hand on the dagger's red leather grip, "it's really just more pretty than anything."

"Oh ho," PepperGarten spun, picked up three of the bowls of berries and greens, carried them to the two guests, and thrust them into their hands, "and what does Edsumar have to say about that? Does it agree with you? I bet it agrees that it's pretty! Eat your grub, you're going to need the strength."

The Kid started popping berries into his mouth, so he didn't have to answer.

"Is it talking to you right now?" PepperGarten whispered conspiratorially, "Is it feeding you information the way PepperGarten feeds you grub?"

"It talks to you?" Esperanza was still staring at the Kid.

"Who you gonna believe?" the Kid mumbled around a mouthful of food, "Me, or a crazy man in the woods?"

"You're in the woods right now, mister," Esperanza snorted, "but fair point. But come on, spill it. With the things I've run across since I got here, a talking knife wouldn't even begin to be the most incredible thing I've seen."

"New here, eh?" PepperGarten cackled. "Thought so, both of you. All three of you. Too dumb to have been here the whole time."

The room grew quiet, and Esperanza and the Kid traded looks.

PepperGarten moved across the room and folded himself into a sitting position beside the fox with his legs crossed. The man began scrubbing the animal behind the ears, then down her side to get her belly.

She fell over to let the man give her belly rubs, making squeaking yips that sounded like laughter.

"You two should talk about this sometime," PepperGarten looked back at his guests, "you know?"

Neither answered, and both concentrated on eating.

"Okay then," the old man said, wiggling his arm that now had a fox kit and ferret attached to it as they grappled for his attention and their own belly rubs, "well, then just remember, and think about if you're staying or if you're leaving when the time comes."

"We can stay?" the Kid said, turning his attention to PepperGarten.

"We can leave?" Esperanza said at the same time.

"Sure," PepperGarten cackled, "we all decide that for ourselves. Just remember, you're here for a reason. And PepperGarten doesn't mean the reason you have when you're here, but the reason you don't have when you're not here."

"What's that even mean?" Esperanza snorted.

PepperGarten grew quiet and still, staring at Esperanza intently.

"That's up to you," the man said.

Cackling, PepperGarten leapt to his feet again, and moved to where Torrence lay.

"This isn't good," the wild man said. "Our third visitor isn't doing well. It seems a bit of the hound master got inside of him."

"What's that mean?" the Kid asked, "and don't say that it's up to me."

"Nope," the old man stood, plucking herbs from terracotta pots and placing them into his other hand. "This one isn't up to you. It's up to him; it's his fight, but PepperGarten will see if PepperGarten can't whip up a little something to help him out."

Ten minutes later, the Kid and Esperanza held the unconscious barbarian's thick, muscled arms as he struggled against the vile tea that PepperGarten poured down his throat.

Torrence fell through the darkness and hit the road hard, landing on his back.

The Shadow Man stood by a car, flipped over on its side in the ditch next to the asphalt. He smiled at the teenager in front of him and then turned towards the vehicle.

"You stay away from that," Torrence yelled, "my dad's in there, and he needs help!"

The figure ignored him and slowly walked around the trunk of the car, his fingers running along the bumper, his nails rasping out the sound of metal on metal.

Torrence charged, wishing he had a weapon, and closed the distance, desperate to get to the thing before it took his father from him again.

He had his sword in his hand. Torrence glanced down for a moment, and then accepted the fact that his two-handed blade was where it belonged, in his firm grip.

The scene shifted, as it often does in dreams and nightmares, with an otherworldly reality of acceptance of the impossible.

Torrence sat at a square wooden table, the sword laying across it, and the Shadow Man in a chair across from him.

"So," the smoke figure hissed, "you do fight, but only for others, and not for yourself."

The space beyond them didn't exist. It was a wall of darkness a meter away, and Torrence thought that if he reached a hand out and touched that negative space, he'd never see that limb again.

"I fight," Torrence spat the words out at the thing. "I've fought all my life. You don't have any idea what I've gone through."

"You fight, do you?" the man was fading, "then you can fight now."

The table disappeared, and the sword was in Torrence's hand. He was in his wheelchair, sitting in the middle of a dirt-floored arena.

The stands were filled with endless wolf-headed fans, howling for blood, and halogen stadium lights shone down on him, blinding him from whatever foe approached.

The morning brought frost, making the grass around the sanctuary crisp and white, gleaming and glittering in the first rays of the sun.

Esperanza stood outside, her robe wrapped tight around her and her arms folded across her breasts against the chill. Her breath misted in front of her.

She stared at the small blade clutched in her hand.

The Kid was still asleep inside, no doubt because he'd stayed up most of the night doing whatever it is he does when everyone else is sleeping.

That crazy old man, PepperGarten, wasn't anywhere to be found, but footprints crushed into the rime led away from his home.

Esperanza dreamt last night.

She'd been in the stands of an arena, a blend of something from ancient Rome and the Superbowl. Shadowy figures that she couldn't make out had surrounded her, and a scared young black man sat in a wheelchair in the center of the dirt.

She couldn't remember much more, but she had flashes of the big fight and the pain that was in it.

She wondered about her own situation, looking at the knife in her hand.

Were both of the people she was with from her world? Was everyone here from Earth? Was this place in her head, as she lay dying from the pills and alcohol, or was it more real than that? Maybe it was hell, but she no longer thought it was her own private punishment.

PepperGarten had said they'd have a chance to leave. Did they get to decide when? Or was it when they died here?

Could she end it right now, with a few simple cuts of her knife? Or was this part of the plan?

She shook her head, her dark hair moving around her face.

It was too much, and Esperanza just couldn't get her head wrapped around it.

She heard the Kid inside, talking to the squirrels and giggling as he said something about someone named Rocky and asking where Bullwinkle was, then began talking about the creature's nuts.

PepperGarten crested the hill in the distance, waved his greenery staff in her direction, and yelled something to her she couldn't hear. But she could make out his pemtie cackle.

Esperanza sighed, shook her head, turned, and went back inside.

The Shadow Man stalked towards Torrence, dragging a huge black sword as wide as a grown man's shoulders with a sloped jagged edge across the sands of the arena.

"Fight," the Shadow Man whispered in an emotionless voice.

"Look at me," Torrence shouted at his foe, "how can I fight like this?"

"Then give up," the Shadow Man said, "die, and make room for the next combatant. To live, you must fight."

Torrence pulled at his sword, dragging the tip through the sand, drawing it across his lap.

"Every day," the thing said, "you must fight. With every ounce of yourself, with every fiber of your being, you must fight."

"What kind of crap is that?" Torrence sat up in his chair. "That sounds like my old coach before a game. That sounds like every therapist I've ever seen. That sounds like complete bidj."

The crowd chanted. The sound started as a low rumble, the words blending and falling over one another.

"Life is a struggle," the Shadow Man said, "and either you rise to face what comes, or you fall to it."

The chanting of the crowd became stronger; it was only one word they were chanting, but Torrence couldn't make it out.

"You continue to fight," the Shadow Man was closer now, and raised his giant ebony weapon above his head in two hands, preparing to cleave Torrence in half, "you will fail the moment you don't fight."

The word the crowd chanted became clear, the one word it repeated over and over again came to Torrence's ears.

"Choose, choose, choose, choose," the forms in the stands intoned, "choose, choose, choose."

"Do you fight," the Shadow Man asked, his mighty weapon swinging downward towards Torrence, "or do you die?"

Torrence pulled his blade up to block the blow.

"We have to go," Torrence sat up blearily, rubbing his head, "we need to go. Now."

The Kid looked up from where he sat, playing with the kits.

Esperanza turned from stitching her robe to look at him.

"Yeah," she nodded, "I guess we do, don't we?"

PepperGarten cackled and leapt down from the root rafters above.

"Yes," the man said excitedly, "PepperGarten knew you'd make it back. You're a strong one, Torrents the Barbarian, and people shall tell tales of your steel for years to come, and not just the steel of your sword, either."

The man danced across the small room, pulling a half dozen sacks from cubby holes and crevasses.

"PepperGarten made you some things!" The man sang, holding the bags up and doing a little jig. "Meals, bandages, and maybe even some poultices in case you do something really pemtie. Again!"

He smiled; his eyes gleamed.

"Now," he said cheerfully, "get the chuz out of PepperGarten's house!"

Chapter 17

The Nine Towers, according to information that Esperanza gave—and she seemed as surprised as the others that she knew these things—were once hidden from prying eyes by enchantments, charms, and illusions to keep the uninitiated and riffraff away.

There was a tower dedicated to each school of magic, and a secret society of knowledge protecting them. Unlike Pantageas, far in the western lands, this university of the arcane had not been open to anyone who had the gold or power to buy their way in.

The three stood on the plains to the east of the Black Wood, to the west of the Frozen Desert, and to the north of the Blue Desert. In the distance, to the northwest, a haze wavered at the base of multiple structures. Mist shifted and wavered in front of them, a thick patch of white covering the ground between them and the buildings.

Six towers reached towards the sky, five of them tall and slim, graceful in their design and architecture. The sixth was short and squat—compared to the others, though it still towered over the campus of buildings at its base—and was the pitch black of the god Onyx, one of the newer gods who'd risen to power less than a century ago. This tower sat in the center of the ruins and rubble of four other towers.

"There'll be magical wards," Esperanza warned, wrapping the thick woolen cloak PepperGarten had given her around her body, "though some may have faded without upkeep, and others may have been triggered by the necromancer and her legion as it made its way to the towers. Are you sure she came here, Torrence?"

"It's Torrents now," the big man said, "and yes, I'm very sure. She headed this direction, and my dreams showed me the towers. It's where the arena was that I told you about."

"Torrence, Torrents," the Kid said, "they sound alike."

"Which name do you go by, Kid?" Torrents asked. "Do you want us to call you the Kid, or the name you used back home? What was that name again? Oh yeah, you won't tell us. You can't even admit that you had a whole other life before this one."

Torrents had changed since he'd woke from his dream. He walked differently, and he talked differently, but the biggest difference was that he was driven. He didn't seem to wander and go with the flow anymore. He had a purpose, and nothing would stop him or come between him and his goal. He was also was a lot snarkier.

The Kid flinched.

"Okay," the Kid said, his tone nonchalant and conflicting with his body language, "you win. Torrents the Barbarian, the hero of the great white north. You and Nanook can hang out together, kick ass and take names."

"You have a smart mouth," Esperanza sneered, "for a kid."

"I might be called the Kid," the Kid said, keeping an atmosphere of cool uncaring wrapped around him, "but I've lived longer, and harder, than both you put together. Okay? Is that enough admission of my previous life? I've dealt with enough bidj, it's nice to have this little vacation of life and death. And I'm loving it, so I don't feel the need to address who I was before this."

The three fell silent, each alone with their own thoughts.

"Do you think Eloise came here to use the towers to strengthen her army?" the Kid plucked at the petals of a flower and looked down as he broke the awkward silence.

"It would make sense," Esperanza answered, staring at the towers in the distance, "if she wanted to build up her power base quickly, that would be one way to do it."

"What do you think is in there?" the Kid pulled another petal free and watched it drift away on the wind.

"Magical artifacts, like your dagger," Esperanza snuck the jab in, "and she could get a ton of them. There may be wards specifically against the undead, but then again, there may only be things to keep the living out since they might have experimented with necromancy here."

"We should go," Torrents said, "standing here isn't accomplishing anything."

He strode forward, not waiting to see if the others would follow.

They did. Esperanza quickly catching up to walk beside Torrents, and the Kid trailing after.

The trio descended into the valley of the Nine Towers, the mists parting before them. As they drew closer to the cluster of buildings, a pressure built around them. The remnants of magic, seen and felt.

Swirling fog coalesced into creatures that darted away from them, or at other times, stared at them as they passed. Whistles and hoots sounded from the tops of the halls and tenements scattered at the outskirts, perhaps belonging to owls and animals they could find anywhere, or they could've been the spirits of familiars and homunculus that once served the residents and students.

They came to an intersection, three-story barrack-like dormitories on one side, and two-story administration buildings on the other. Ahead of them stood the courtyard that the towers had once surrounded. Overgrown shrubberies—still tended by magical contraptions hovering in the air, their shears too dull to trim back the vegetation—were scattered around the open-air park.

Broken bodies of the undead littered the intersection, showing the marks of mystical energies along their withered flesh. Sooty score marks of flame marred the surrounding ground.

"I guess something reacted to the undead," the Kid said.

"She could still be here," Esperanza whispered.

"Why would she still be here?" the Kid scoffed, raising his voice a little to show he wasn't concerned. "She had a day and a half head start on us."

"Because you don't get all of the magic arsenal a place like this holds in one day." Esperanza's voice was disdainful.

"Also," Torrents said quietly, "an army moves slow, and we move fast."

"The living dead don't need rest breaks," the Kid said.

"Even though an undead army doesn't need to rest," Esperanza said, forgetting to be snarky, "the necromancer does. It takes a lot of energy to keep hundreds of these things in line and moving in the same direction. So, it makes sense that she might still be here."

"Unless she just came for one thing," Torrents interrupted, pointing at the Tower of Onyx.

The other two looked in the direction Torrents indicated.

The massive black tower dominated more than a quarter of the courtyard, the four towers from which it had seemingly grown acting as legs for its raised form. The other five towers stood tall and still beautiful behind the dark, stout fortification.

Underneath the Tower of Onyx, and all around its base, were at least three score broken forms from the necromancer's legion. An altar in the center of the shadow of the structure above it glowed with a purple aura, green lightnings arcing through it.

A single figure, shrouded in a dark mist, stood underneath it, looking straight at the trio.

Torrents drew his blade and charged in the same movement, moving across the gardens.

"No," Esperanza cried, reaching for the man, "damn fool barbarian, he'll get himself killed."

"And us with him," the Kid added, also moving forward.

The street thief darted to one side, finding cover behind bushes, and shouted over his shoulder to Esperanza, "Do you want to live forever? There can be only one!"

Esperanza huffed, and walked forward slowly, her hands working in front of her as if she were kneading an invisible ball of dough. Silver light sprung into being within the confines of her hands, growing larger as she worked it.

The barbarian reached his target, swinging his sword in an arc, only to have it pass through the figure.

The form in front of him laughed, a familiar voice behind it.

"You're a pemtie," Eloise said, "and you shall die for your pemtieity."

"Nuh uh, Eloise," the Kid said, stepping out of the shadows behind the necromancer, flinging his white-bladed dagger at her, "you are, and you will."

The blade hit the figure and slowed when it passed through her, a line of blood showing as the illusion of the necromancer wavered and shimmered.

The woman in the image screamed and clutched at the small of her back where the weapon had hit her phantasm.

"I am not Eloise, foolish child," the necromancer screamed in anger, spinning to face the Kid, "I am Aku'ji, Mistress of Death, and Wielder of Woe. And I have the scepter of Necropties, and shall have more power over the dead than any of you can imagine!"

The image hesitated, looking towards the Dragon's Dagger on the cobblestone path in front of her.

"How did you get that dagger?" she demanded. "How did you capture the spirit of a Dragon Lord? Why does Edsumar serve you?"

"Really?" said the Kid, hands on his hips, "Does everyone know about this damn thing?"

"Give it to me!" Aku'ji shouted. "It will serve me!"

"Suck my left nut, bitch," the Kid said nonchalantly and edged forward, his wavy sword held ready.

The necromancer threw both hands outward, one towards the Kid and the other towards Torrents.

A bolt of white-hot energy shot towards each.

The Kid dodged to one side, his sword taking the brunt of the blow and bending into a curled and twisted shape as it melted in his hand. He shouted, dropped the weapon, and clutched his scorched hand.

Torrents took the bolt in the center of his chest, and flew backwards, rolling heels over head and coming up on his feet. His torso smoldered, but not as much as his glare did, as he refocused on the woman.

"Wait!" Esperanza commanded, stepping beside the barbarian. Then more gently, she said, "I've got this."

The silver globe of energy was the size of a beach ball now, humming with a tinkling noise. Esperanza thrust her hands forward and the magical sphere slowly advanced, growing larger, winds and lightning exploding to life within it.

"Nobody hurts my friends," Esperanza growled.

The necromancer waved her hands and brought them together in a 'X' shape in front of her, her own magics coming to life as black swirling fog and green sparks.

The silver globe met the magics of the necromancer, and the two forces burst into a blast of silver and green.

The Kid dropped to the ground, covering his head with his arms. Torrents threw up an arm to guard his eyes, but Esperanza just watched calmly, her globe encompassing and swallowing the necromancer.

The silver sphere pulsed.

"We've got her!" the Kid shouted, leaping to his feet and pumping a fist in the air.

"Not quite," Esperanza said through clenched teeth, her face tight with concentration, "that's an illusion that she's pushing magic through."

Esperanza spoke in short, broken phrases through the effort of the magic she used.

"But I think," the priestess continued, "I might…be able…to do a little something…with it…while we…have her essence trapped."

The sphere shrank, growing smaller with each panting breath that Esperanza took.

Torrents gripped his charred chest with one hand and held his sword ready with the other.

Esperanza stood, feet spread apart, and shoulders hunched over her hands, working them around an imaginary ball, pushing it smaller and smaller. The larger globe surrounding the necromancer's illusion mirrored the effect.

The whole thing collapsed, and Esperanza's hands came together with a clapping noise.

"She got away?" Torrents growled.

"She was never here," the Kid snatched the dagger he'd thrown from the ground where it had landed, "that was an illusion."

"But I think," Esperanza stood with her hands on her knees, panting, "your dagger stopped her from escaping right away, and I got something from the magical prison I caught her in. A place, maybe. I might know where she was when she did this."

"So," Torrents said, holding his freshly blistering wound, "you know where we need to go?"

"Not quite." Esperanza moved to the big man, peeled his arm away from the injury, and inspected the area. "But I have an impression, and I think PepperGarten might know where we should go. Now, hold still, I think this is going to require one of that crazy, old man's infamous poultices before we try to travel."

"I'll keep an eye out for ghosts and goblins, while you do that, then. And what kind of name is Aku'ji anyway?" the Kid asked, "Is that supposed to be scary or something?"

"That's something coming from someone who goes by 'the Kid'" Torrents grimaced under Esperanza's ministrations.

"Yeah?" the Kid said, "Well, quiet down Torrents, because your name isn't quite a winner either."

Esperanza smirked as the two men bickered.

Chapter 18

"So, we could've gotten a magic sword or something from that black tower?" Torrents asked as PepperGarten checked the burns on his chest.

It had been almost five days since the three had left PepperGarten's sanctuary. They'd departed the Nine Towers within the hour after bandaging Torrents's wound and had traveled until dark before setting camp and watch. That night had brought the northern lights, a dazzling display that Torrents said made him think of the equalizer on his sound software.

Esperanza had said it was God's equalizer.

The next day brought clear skies and swarms of tiny biting gnats. After much cajoling from the Kid, Esperanza reluctantly called upon the power of Latress to sweep the pests away. The rest of the day passed with no other trouble, and Torrents took a few minutes to show the Kid how to use a bow. It took over ten arrows, but the Kid brought down a hare, and the three shared a dinner of roasted coney and some tubers that PepperGarten had supplied before they'd left.

They'd arrived the following day at the odd man's domicile, just before lunchtime. PepperGarten had a simmering pot of vegetable stew brewing over a large fire outside of his home. He'd been sitting on a tree stump carved into a chair, stirring the soup with a wooden stick that still had leaves sprouting from it, when they'd arrived.

"You could have," PepperGarten answered the barbarian's question absentmindedly, "but you would've left with a lot more than a weapon. When those towers first started cropping up across all of Teurone, maybe even all of Aetheria, they gave out magical goodies to anyone who wanted one, but only one per person. But they always came with a hook in them. PepperGarten's heard too many tales about someone who accepted such a thing, and it came back to bite them in the ass, eventually."

The Kid sat cross-legged on the floor with the three fox kits playing tag on his lap and around his back, nipping at his fingers and he feinted, grabbing them.

Esperanza was leaning back on the small bed of clover that Torrents had slept in last time they were here. She was fiddling with her holy symbol of Latress, turning it over and over in her hands while staring at it.

"Okay, that should do it," the little man finished wrapping the barbarian's wound and slapped the big man in the middle of his chest and giggled.

The barbarian winced and held his hand to the area.

"Can I ask now?" Esperanza said from where she sat, not looking up from what she was doing.

"No need," PepperGarten said, "you've already asked. You don't need to repeat yourself. You said you had the feeling of green, moisture, moving in slow motion, and the smell of natural rot. But also, as if there were something, not threatening, but not helpful, watching you. Yes, PepperGarten thinks PepperGarten knows the place."

The small man hopped to his feet and twisted his hips to a rhythm in his own head as he danced across the room.

"He reminds me of Ed Grimly when he does that." The Kid said, only to receive confused looks from Esperanza and Torrents. "Never mind, before your time."

"PepperGarten remembers that," the old man said as he plucked apples from a bowl and debated which one to eat. "PepperGarten also remembers the copier guy, and the liar guy. Those were good times."

"You know our world?" the Kid stopped playing with the animals and turned to look at their host, as did the others. "Have you been there?"

"There, here," the odd fellow bit into his chosen apple, answering between chewing, "not much difference, same thing, but different."

"Great," Esperanza sighed, "more things that make no sense."

"It makes sense once you know what it means," PepperGarten said, smiling widely, "but PepperGarten thinks it's more important for you to go east and find the Preserving Fluids."

"That sounds disgusting," the Kid said, "perhaps even a little horrifying."

"Is it dangerous?" Torrents pulled a fresh shirt over his head. It was scratchy, but it covered him well enough.

"Everything is dangerous," PepperGarten answered, "if you do not know what you need to know."

Esperanza sighed again.

"What information will you give us that would be helpful in this?" the Kid said through gritted teeth. "Directions? A list of monsters?"

"PepperGarten will tell you this," the old man put his fingertips on temples, and squinted, "remember who you are, what brought you to this point, and who you want to be, and you might make it out."

"Is that a prophecy?" Torrents asked, "Is that why you put your fingers to your head? Some sort of psychic power?"

"No," the small man answered, "I just like how the colors blur when I do that!"

They'd crossed the thinnest part of the Blue Desert and entered the western reaches of the Upper Swamp without incident. It had taken two days, and they set camp a few kilometers into the bog.

Small hillocks rose from ankle deep water and tall grass. The sounds of crickets and frogs, in their final mating frenzy before winter, filled the evening air as they cooked their meal of some sort of lizard that hadn't run when they'd approached.

"I guess these things aren't used to humans around here," the Kid turned a makeshift spit over the open fire, "and didn't know to run when we showed up."

"Or it's poisonous," Torrents said blandly.

The Kid's head jerked up to look at the man.

A smile crept onto the barbarian's face.

"What?" the Kid said, leaning forward. "Is that a smile? Did the big bad barbarian make a joke?"

"Your face is the joke here," the big man said, his grin huge now.

"Lame," Esperanza chimed in, "if you guys are gonna make a bromance, please be more clever and entertaining for those of us who are forced to watch it. How long until our mutant iguana entrée is ready? The potatoes are done, and the berries will ferment if we have to wait much longer."

"It's not like back home, is it?" Torrents smiled again. "Back there, everything cooked quicker. Even over a campfire because we had metal walls, or pots, or grates to cook with."

"Oh, the good old days," the Kid sighed and turned the spit again, "before we were surrounded by all this nature and junk."

"You know," Esperanza said, leaning back against a spindly tree, "at first, I missed my phone and always having something to do. Now though, I kinda like it. It's more, peaceful without all the technology. It's like we have more time to be who we really are without worrying about the rest of the world's opinion about us and what we're doing."

"Yeah," Torrents agreed, "I definitely like watching the branches above me sway, and staring at the stars as I fall asleep. You know there was a meteor shower last night? I don't think I'd ever seen one before. I mean, I heard they were happening, on the news, online, or from someone during the day, but I never actually just went outside and looked up to see one happen."

"I did," the Kid said. "When I was young, my brothers would camp out in the backyard, for it seemed like half the summer when school was out. I'd go out there with them, and this was before there were streetlights everywhere, and you could really see the stars, just like we do here, now."

"Before streetlights? How old are you?" Torrents asked, "Or were you, you know, back there?"

"Let's just say, my mother was a war bride," the Kid laughed.

"Which war?" Esperanza asked, "Desert Storm? Vietnam? Korean War?"

"No," the Kid chuckled again, "World War II."

Silence fell across the trio as the Kid watched the sun set over the mountains to the west, then glanced to the east to see the deep indigo of night advancing across the sky, stars popping into his awareness like tiny white fireflies.

Torrents and Esperanza stared at the Kid, then exchanged glances.

"Okay, yeah," Esperanza said, "I guess you do have a little more experience than us."

The Kid shrugged.

"Unless he's lying about it," Torrents said.

The Kid shrugged again.

"I don't think it matters anymore," the Kid turned the spit again, "not here. This is a second chance at life, no matter how much, or how little, of your old life you lived."

Torrents and Esperanza both took a double meaning from that simple statement, though neither knew the other also felt a deep pang of regret, mixed with excitement and hope.

They ate dinner mostly in silence, occasionally pointing out something to the others. A shooting star, a raccoon in the underbrush who smelled the food, a swarm of actual fireflies dancing in the distance, and other things that they'd never taken the time to notice before. The night filled with the noise of the traffic of the wilderness. Night birds called, frogs sang the song of their people, insects chirruped, and distant predators called to one another.

The three settled down into their routine, Torrents finding a place where he could whittle some of the smaller firewood while watching the camp. The Kid bedded down, falling asleep almost immediately. Esperanza whispered prayers to her god, which seemed worlds away, and even muttered a short thanks to Latress for her protection.

The night moved, the stars spinning across the sky, and when Torrents went to stand to wake the Kid for his watch, he found a thick gelatinous layer of liquid covered his feet.

The barbarian thought he should be concerned by this, but it didn't trouble him. The viscous coating lulled him, and it felt warm and comforting.

Looking at his companions, he saw the same substance surrounding most of their bodies, even though they were atop a knoll and the water couldn't reach them.

Esperanza's eyes were still open, and she stared dreamily upward into the heavens, as if having a pleasant daydream. She was lower on the hill than the Kid, who was curled up next to the fire.

Torrents watched in dazed contentment as the clear ooze crept further up the priestess's prone form. It moved across her thighs, and then belly, in slow undulating movements, like high tide coming in on a calm lake. He watched it coat her shoulders, run across her neck, and then up her breasts. It moved across her face last, pooling in the hollows of her open eyes, then filling her nostrils, and her mouth. Soon the woman was completely cocooned in the stuff, and Torrents watched her breathing slow until it was imperceptible, and he couldn't be sure if she was breathing at all.

Slowly turning his head, disturbing the sluggish creep of the ooze working up his neck towards his own face, he saw the Kid was also being enveloped. The stuff had already made its way onto the Kid's shoulders, the highest part of the street thief who laid on his side, and was working towards the prone man's face. It slid smoothly down the shoulder into the crook of the Kid's neck, then began its leisurely journey up the side of his face to fill in his features with a thin sheen of translucent emulsion. The Kid's breathing slowed to a stop as well.

Any of this did not disturb Torrents. It didn't feel dangerous, and no part of him sensed anything that would harm them. He slowly smiled and breathed a deep sigh as the ooze made its way across his own eyes, blurring his vision, before moving to his nose and mouth. As it found its way into his final orifices, he drifted away.

Chapter 19

Jen sat in an armchair, the kind with the little wings near the head, high arms, and that ugly, blotchy material that reminded her of colonial days. It was her favorite, having belonged to her grandmother. Handed down for generations, Jen didn't know who she'd hand it down to, because her son had died over twenty-five years ago.

She missed him terribly, even if she couldn't remember much about him anymore. Mothers were supposed to miss their children, even after they were gone and forgotten by the rest of the world. She remembered that he'd been over thirty when he died. Thirty-two? She couldn't remember, and her mind wouldn't wrap itself around the math tonight, not with the meds and the treatments.

She was just so tired. Why would the treatments be almost as bad as the cancer itself? She'd struggled all her life. Why did she have to continue straight up to her death?

Jen had started working when she was twelve, just babysitting, nothing hard. She'd gotten a job at the local diner when she was fifteen, and kept working up to two years ago, when she got too sick to keep a job.

But she had things in her life to keep her going. Things like Cuddles, her dog. She didn't know where he was right now. Maybe the in-home care nurse— what was her name? Oh yeah, it was Marjorie, or

Margaret, or something like that—had taken Cuddles for a walk.

Something nagged at her though, even as sleep pulled her down. It was the thought that she wasn't old anymore. She was just a kid now. She was The Kid.

She had a new life, one that wasn't constant pain of achy joints that stabbed at her when she ran her hands under water that was too cold. One where she didn't have to stand up slowly, because her knees might give out.

She felt the gentle, warm tug of sleep pulling at her again, and she wanted to just relax and remember.

But another small voice told her that she had another life, and it was a different world.

Esperanza had nothing. She had a job, but she hated it. Hate may have been too strong of a word, but the job did nothing for her. She had no reason, other than the little bit of money it gave her to survive on, to go to that place another single day.

She had an apartment, it was in the city, and close to everything. But that didn't matter when you couldn't afford to do anything. And she didn't have any friends.

Sure, she knew people, and she called them friends. But would they answer if she called at three forty-six in the morning, she wondered, glancing at the time in the corner of her computer screen?

She didn't want to hang out with her family. Her mother or grandmother just nagged at her about things she didn't do, and disapproved of the things she did. Nothing she did was good enough for them. They told her that by now, in her late twenties, she should at least have a man, if not a couple of babies. Esperanza could barely afford her car payments and utilities. How could she afford to date, let alone raise a family?

And her sisters and brothers were living their own lives. They each had their own problems, most of them living with someone or married already, or going to college like the youngest. Esperanza's father kept asking why she hadn't gone to college, and reminded her she could still go, and even offered to help pay for it. But he was already working two jobs to put his other kids through college. Why should she burden him with more?

She looked at the bottle of antidepressants the doctor had prescribed her. It sat next to the bottle of cheap vodka. It was the same brand she'd used to drink with her friends behind the gas station when she was still in high school. It was rot gut, the cheap shit, and only good for cleaning rust out of the pipes. But it would do the trick.

A small, strange knife sat beside them. She knew it didn't belong here, but it held her gaze for a moment.

Would anyone even notice if she did this? Would anyone even miss her?

She looked out the window as the wind picked up, and it seemed to call her name.

Torrence was back in the arena, and the crowd was going wild. Dozens of Shadow Men were on their knees, clutching their heads at the noise of cheering.

Torrence turned a slow circle, looking at the crowd that kept the shadows of his past from attacking him. The shadow things shifted through faces and bodies, each one looking like someone he knew, loved, hated, argued with, fought with, cried to, or interacted with in some close and personal way at some point.

More shadowy figures were climbing over the walls of the arena, but the sound of the cheering crowd blocked them from getting in. It created a bubble of space, and the shades scrambled along the invisible dome, blacking out the open sky above the stadium.

Once all the overhead area was covered, the darkness of the shapes thickened above Torrence, and the sound of the crowd was dampened and felt slightly muted. The pressure in the air increased; a pounding in Torrence's head drummed in time with it, keeping the beat as it blocked out the encouragement of the spectators of his mind.

Jen was in court. Her husband of fifteen years sat across the table from her, smiling. He'd get his way. He'd be allowed to leave the marriage, and pay her thirty dollars a month, because she had a job and brought in enough money that he didn't need to pay alimony, just that little bit of child support.

The seventies were a decade of progressive thinking, following the free spirit roots set in the sixties. Women were equals, at least that's what they were told. But here she sat, getting screwed one last time by the man that wanted out.

Her nine-year-old son was at her sister's house, waiting for his mother and father to come home and tell him everything would okay. And his father would do that, down on one knee so he could look his son in the eye, and one hand on the kid's shoulder to let him know everything'll be alright. Daddy just needs to go away for a little while, and find himself. Find himself with the help of Linda, the blonde waitress that works in the same diner that Jen had worked in as a teenager, and who now works as the secretary in the used car lot that Jen had helped pay for when it was getting started.

She had to live life, if for no other reason than to live because her son died.

Aw, come on, Kid, someone said to Jen, and it felt like whoever it was had been standing right over her shoulder.

Don't fall for this shit, Kid, the voice urged, *you're better than this. I didn't choose you because you'd just roll over and die—and in this case, die over and over again—to feed some sort of swamp slug.*

Jen looked over her left shoulder, and then over her right one.

"Who is that?" Jen asked, but no one at the table seemed to notice the question. In fact, everyone at the table appeared to be getting a bit out of focus and growing wispy and faint, like they were dissipating.

That's it, Kid, the voice almost shouted into Jen's head. *Come back to me. You got this, and we got things that need to be done. Kick this thing's ass, or mind, and let's get going.*

Esperanza moved to the window and pulled on it to open it, but it wouldn't budge. Memories called to her from behind, pulling at her, begging her to come back, to nurture and care for them. But the wind called as well.

The storm rumbled, distant and fleeting, the noise almost drowned out by the fog of the pills, alcohol, and memories of her life.

Esperanza jerked on the window again, trying to tug it open. It creaked under her effort and slid up about a hand's width.

She dropped her hands down, turning them palm up, and gripped the underside of the window. She put one foot on the windowsill, and then hunched her shoulders and pulled upward. The window resisted and jerked down.

Gritting her teeth, tears coming to her eyes, Esperanza gave one last effort to open this window. The tears were frustration, anger, sadness, and all the things that called to her from the small room behind her.

The wind sang outside, singing of opportunities, freedoms, and adventure that made life so much more than the same doldrums every day, in and out.

The window lurched open, and Esperanza ducked through it and rolled out onto the fire escape. She looked back at the knife on the table for a moment before turning back to the landing.

Laughing, she grabbed the railing and ran upward, taking the steps two at a time. She doubled back when she hit the next landing and took the next flight at an even more reckless speed.

When she ran out of stairs to climb, and she realized she had made it to the roof. The wind wound around her like some giant, unseen cat, glad she'd finally came home.

The breeze pulled at clothes that hadn't been there before; the constraining clothes she's worn all her life had been replaced with flowing robes in hues of pinks, purples, and white. The sleeves, cut with lace to resemble feathers, hung down her sides when she raised her arms.

She was on a riverbed now, made of flat, rounded stones. The water trickled, rippling in the dancing wind.

Esperanza held her arms above her, raising her face to the sky; a small ball of energy forming a few meters in front of her.

It expanded, and Esperanza laughed in delight.

It grew, becoming a globe, then a large orb of shifting grays, with red and purple energy breaking through, making it look like cracks in the sphere.

She thrust her arms forward, and the wind rushed past her towards the magical, circular creation; it lifted and was flung away.

The caressing gusts lifted her into the air, swirling upward, wrapping her in its cool embrace. And then Esperanza was flying.

She sailed across the sky, looking down on the world below. All her worries, fears, and life pressures were so small and far away. She was above it all and never wanted to be stuck in that mire again.

She was free.

Torrents woke. He blinked, but there was something in his eyes. Someone's hands scraped at something on his skin, his nose, and mouth. He coughed, sputtering, and felt a thick phlegm rise from his throat and collect in a jelly-like lump in his mouth. He spat it out, leaning forward as he did.

Hands thumped his back, and voices spoke to him. They seemed to be very far away, or as if he was underwater. The sounds were muddled and muted.

"Okay, alright, stop," Torrents said hoarsely, spitting out more of the goo, holding his hands up to wave the helping hands away, "give me a second, let me catch my breath."

The hands moved away. Torrents squeegeed out his ears, one at a time, with a finger. Putting a finger to the side of his nose, he blew the gunk inside it onto the grass between his knees. He scraped the remaining ooze from his face.

Looking around, he saw Esperanza and the Kid standing in front of him, one on each side. It was full daylight, and from the position of the sun, it was almost noon.

His skin burned from the contact with the gelatinous liquid. He scraped at it, sloughing it off onto the grass.

"Here," the Kid said, holding a small cooking pot full of water towards him, "this might help. There's a rag in there, too. Take a moment to get more water if you need to."

"Thanks," Torrents stumbled to his feet, then swayed.

Esperanza's hands caught him by the elbow and armpit.

"Take it slow," the priestess smiled, "it takes a few minutes for the effects of that thing to wear off."

"You're smiling," Torrents said, confused. "Why are you smiling? You never smile."

"Don't be an asshole," Esperanza swatted Torrents's bicep with the hand that was holding his elbow. "Just go and get cleaned up. We have an undead army to track down."

Chapter 20

The muck and mire bubbled, hundreds of dead bodies rising to their feet as one. Acres of shallow, stagnant water moved as the necromancer, Aku'ji, called upon the dark powers at her disposal. The smell of rotting flesh blended with the fetid air of the Upper Swamp.

Necromancy wasn't its own type of magic. It manipulated all five magics. It called upon elemental magics to transport the energy needed to animate the dead. It interacted with the alchemical magics, converting dead flesh to a state between what it was, and what is now is, allowing the dead to replenish themselves in ways the living could not. It conjured the cold, ethereal energies, and motes of darkness to strike the core within the dead, and give them animation. It pulled on the holy magics of the gods, drawing from their realms of faith, and bestowing the fears and beliefs of the living to give the dead the strength to walk. And lastly, it drew upon the casters own mind magics to control the things that rose to walk again after death.

A circle of over five hundred corpses, fresh and old, surrounded the rising army within the swamp. These had been gathered from caravan trains, small villages, or even lone travelers, since the Day of Phāz six years ago—the mystical day that came every four years and fell between the old year and the new.

It was pure luck that Aku'ji had come across a horde of plainsmen, warriors of the north, just a few weeks ago, and was able to catch them unaware enough to bring them into her dark fold.

But this wasn't the first time she'd gathered an army. It wasn't the second, either. She'd been dabbling in the necromantic arts for over sixty years. She felt the surge of power when the Talisman—the rogue comet that fell into orbit above the world for a decade or more—hung in the sky. She saw the other necromancers scramble for the power that the Talisman rained down upon the land.

She watched, and she waited.

The others fought each other, and all of them fought against Rondarius the Foul. The Master Necromancer had been trapped in some forgotten keep deep in Land's End. But when demons had been released upon the land, Rondarius had escaped his stone prison that hadn't been more than three paces wide. When the magical radiation of the comet fell upon the land, Rondarius rose to power, crushing heroes and decimating kingdoms with equal recklessness.

Aku'ji had found her way into the demon-infested land while war raged with armies of undead to the north and west. She found Rondarius's hidden library, and though it seemed he'd boiled most of his leather-bound tomes to survive his imprisonment, she found enough information to rise in power beyond most necromancer's dreams.

Letting the others kill one another off, she waited.

Now was the time. Humans, aeifain, rokairn, and other humanoids had repopulated after the Downfall, and were a ripe crop ready for harvesting.

She'd built her army three times over, and each time brought them here to the Upper Swamp, where a symbiotic creature fed off living creatures placed in stasis. Here, she used this non-sentient being to store her armies in a place they wouldn't attract attention and wouldn't rot while they waited.

And now she called them forth once again, the Scepter of Necropties in her upraised hand.

And they answered.

"Oh, hell naw," Esperanza said, as the three lay on their bellies, hidden by an overgrown deadfall.

They'd searched the bogs, working their way to the east, for three days before finding evidence of the dead army's passage.

The fen swallowed such signs quickly.

Now, they lay on a small hill overlooking the massive exhumation of a force that would triple the size of the necromancer's military.

The Kid had his hands cupped into twin tubes and held them to his eyes like a pair of imaginary binoculars.

Torrents stared at him, a smile quirking at the corners of his mouth.

"You know," Torrents said to the Kid, "the pemtie things you do are much more amusing now that I know you were more than three times my age."

"They work," the Kid said, pulling his hands from his eyes, and held them towards the barbarian, "wanna try?"

"Spoiler alert! It's his magic," Esperanza said, "now can we get back to discussing this suicide mission? Been there, done that, literally, don't need another t-shirt."

"So," the Kid leaned around Torrents to look at Esperanza, "you think we should just skedaddle and open up this world's first Starbucks? I thought this was why we were here."

"Well," Esperanza squirmed, "it is, but come on, how do we even begin to take something like this down?"

"Same way we eat an elephant," the Kid replied, turning back to peer through his hand binoculars again.

Esperanza looked across at the Kid, her head cocked, and her face confused.

"One bite at a time," Torrents said, and Esperanza glanced at him, "that's how you eat an elephant. One bite at a time."

"What the hell does that even mean in this situation?" Esperanza threw her hands up. "I'm not biting one of those things."

Both Torrents and the Kid were studying the raising of the army, which appeared to be almost completed, and didn't answer.

"That was a joke," Esperanza sighed, "you know, ha, ha, funny?"

"Torrents," the Kid jabbed the big guy with his elbow, and pointed, "you see that down there?"

Esperanza and Torrents both looked towards where the Kid indicated.

A group of newly raised dead had been corralled together, and four forms circled them likes wolves surrounding a foal. The thin dark figures that had wrangled the six pale figures into a tight knot launched themselves into the huddle. They tore and ripped at the recently reborn undead.

"What're they doing?" the Kid mumbled.

"They're feeding on the weak," Torrents answered, "to make themselves stronger."

"Really?" the Kid glanced towards the big man.

"Pretty much." Esperanza watched the slaughter with interest. "Necromancy only has so much energy to go around. For something to become a more powerful undead creature, they need to get the extra, for lack of a better word, nutrition from somewhere. And I assume this is how you get things like the super-fast, hissing thing Torrents told us about meeting when he was traveling with Axle, or the hound master, or other such things."

"What about vampires, banshees, or ghosts?" the Kid asked.

"No," Esperanza shook her head slowly, "I don't think so. I think those things are a different process, because they have complete free will and autonomy. Aku'ji may have some of those, but I doubt it. They take focused will to control. Most necromancers just work in tandem with them, rather than trying to dominate them."

"How the hell," Torrents asked, "do you know so much about necromancy?"

"It's this body," Esperanza shrugged. "It used to study diseases and the undead, hunting both and destroying them, and it still has all that knowledge stored inside it. Just like you and your skill with the sword, or the Kid and his illusions and backflips and all that shit. I have access to what was already here."

"So, you're like an avenging angel?" the Kid asked.

Any answer Esperanza had was lost as a sound rose from behind them, the sound of a small log snapping in half.

They turned as one.

An enormous man, or a small giant, stood over them.

He was over three meters tall, dressed in uncured furs, and his bare torso and face covered with mounds of warts and moles that grew on top of one another. The sound had been of him tearing a limb as thick as Torrents's thigh from the deadfall.

The giant swung it around and then hit it three or four times against a fallen tree to clear the loose bark. He held it up, inspecting his new club.

Torrents rolled to his feet and brought his sword up in one movement. With both hands on the hilt, he thrust forward at chest height, and the sword slid into the belly of the giant.

The behemoth looked down, squinting at the blade in his gut.

"Dead me doesn't hurt," the huge man grunted in broken language. "Magic woman make it hurt no more. But says I eat you, and I want to eat you, and make her happy. Now you can go die."

Grabbing the blade of the sword in one huge mitt, the colossus pulled it free of his midsection, slicing his hand open in the process. No blood welled from either wound, merely a thick black ichor beaded at the openings.

With his other hand, the immense man swung his club upward, and Torrents stepped to one side to avoid it. But the blow wasn't meant for him. The tree trunk swept past, connecting with Esperanza and the dead trees above her.

The woman tumbled backwards, over the crest of the hill, and down the other side to land face down in the muck below.

The deadfall shuddered, logs falling around the two remaining men, and rolling down every side of the hill they'd been hiding on.

"Get to her," Torrents growled to the Kid, dancing around the falling timbers, "I'll keep this guy busy."

The Kid rolled to one side to avoid a shattered trunk that landed where he'd been a moment before, got to his feet and leapt on top of a rolling log, jumped to another, and threw himself into the air toward where Esperanza had flown.

Flipping, with the help of a mental push of his own magics, he landed in front of the prone form of the priestess on one knee, and one fist planted into the ground as he constructed a solid shield of mental energy.

Falling trunks crashed into it, and the physical force of the mass pushed him back, sliding his whole body along the mud and soft ground until it touched Esperanza. The shield shattered under the onslaught and the Kid took a face full of splinters.

The Kid reached down, grabbing the priestess by the collar of her cloak and pulled her face from the thick swamp water. Strings of dark vegetation hung from her.

Sticky sacks flew from the hidden recesses of the broken deadfall and landed around the two, rupturing. Hundreds of spiders the size of a man's fist poured from the broken web bags as the baby arachnids were forced into the world.

"Oh, bidj," the Kid said, looking around, "if the babies are this big, I wonder what the adults look like."

As if in response to his curiosity, three hairy eight-legged, creatures the size of ponies scurried down the hillside towards him and his unconscious companion.

"Oh," the Kid sighed and drew his dagger, "me and big mouth."

Chapter 21

Torrents jabbed with his sword, and the hulk in front of him caught it with his sliced hand, three fingers bending backwards, bones snapping.

The goliath swung his club with a roar, and Torrents rolled to avoid the blow. The ground shuddered as the tree trunk narrowly missed the warrior.

Getting to his feet, the barbarian thrusted again, cutting into the massive thigh of his foe. Torrents shoved the weapon forward, tearing the flesh more than cutting it, and the giant fell to one knee.

The club caught the warrior in his ribs. Torrents stumbled to the side, hearing a cracking noise as the wind went out of him.

His next breath shot stabbing pain through his chest. Steadying himself, he prepared for the next strike, raising his sword overhead. The blow slammed into his weapon, blocked, but sending Torrents to one knee under the force of it.

Twisting his blade, the barbarian turned the club away, and it hit the ground beside him. Reversing the blade, he stabbed up and the sword bit into the throat of the colossus. Torrents pushed, sliding the steel through the creature's neck and out the back.

The titan jerked away, standing on his one good leg, and the sword ripped free of the barbarian's grip.

Torrents dropped to the ground, steadied himself with his hands, and kicked out. His foot met the giant's knee, and he heard a satisfying crunch.

The hulk lurched backwards, his club dropping from his hands as he fell on his butt with both legs disabled.

The sword wobbled in the fleshy sheath of the monster's neck, tearing it open further. The undead creature didn't gasp, not needing to breathe.

Torrents stood and surveyed the situation. He needed his sword to finish his foe, but the beast's flailing hands stopped him from approaching to recover it.

He clutched his side, and stooping and grunting with pain, the barbarian hefted his enemy's club. Shuffling forward, Torrents bashed at the handle of his own sword, twisting it in the thing's throat. The head lolled to one side, partially severed from its shoulders.

Torrents heaved a sigh, wincing at the deep breath, then pummeled his foe's arms and chest until it lay still, limbs broken, and ribs shattered.

The giant lay disabled, but still trying to gain its feet.

Recovering his own weapon, Torrents finished the grisly task.

Leaning heavily on the sword, the barbarian turned to look for his companions.

The Kid dragged Esperanza's unconscious form onto the solid ground of the hill where they'd watched the undead army.

A quick glance over his shoulder told the Kid that the army in question was mobilizing and moving away in ragged lines.

The small spiders scurried over the priestess's body and up the Kid's arms. The rogue dropped his friend and began swiping at the arachnids, knocking a dozen from his arms and chest.

The three adults swarmed towards him. He was unsure if they were protecting the babies, or just out for an easy meal, but he drew Edsumar and stood over his friend.

The lead spider closed on the Kid.

"Edsumar," the Kid mumbled, shaking his dagger as if to wake the dragon spirit inside of it, "if you have any awesome powers, now would be a good time to reveal them."

You're doing great, Edsumar said in the Kid's head. *Keep up the good work.*

The Kid slashed at the beast when it came within reach. It reared up, emitting a hiss.

The blade missed.

"Oh great," the Kid said, "they hiss. That's chuzzing terrifying. I didn't like them when they were the size of my fingernail, and I really don't like them now."

The hairy legs stroked the air, the head raised, and the monster looked for an opening. The other two caught up, and the three formed a half circle around the Kid.

"At least they don't have pack tactics," the Kid grunted, and hurled the dagger at the one lunging at him.

The blade flew with unerring accuracy and sunk deep into the head of the lead spider. The thing bucked, launching itself three meters straight up.

"And they chuzzing jump, too?" the Kid shrieked, "Oh my chuzzing god, can this get any worse?"

That's when he realized he was now weaponless, and the other two were charging towards him.

"When will I learn," the Kid dove to one side, trying to draw the giant creatures away from the unconscious priestess.

Chelicerae dug into the Kid's thigh, tearing into the flesh and withdrawing, leaving two pencil-sized holes in his leg.

The Kid screamed, flailing at the thing and wishing he had his dagger back. Then the magical weapon was back in his hand, and he was slashing wildly at the creature's exposed face.

Half the spider's head dropped to the grass, neatly severed. The Kid stabbed forward, and the blade cut a deep gash across the multifaceted eyes.

I can always find you, Edsumar said, *if you're close enough*.

"You think you could've mentioned this sooner?" the Kid said through gritted teeth.

You never asked, the dagger answered.

The Kid took a step, and the leg with the bite wound gave out, dropping him to the ground.

"In that case," he said, carefully pushing to his feet, "can you remove venom or heal that leg?"

Don't be silly, Edsumar said, *I'm just a dagger*.

"Right," the Kid threw the dagger again.

It sunk into the abdomen of the blinded spider and burst out the other side. The creature did a frantic dance sideways, and fell, curling its legs underneath its body and cartwheeled down the hillside.

The dagger appeared in his hand again, and he prepared to throw it at the last target, who stood a few meters away, front legs waving in the air in a striking pose and hissing.

The Kid's vision blurred, and he knew the venom was coursing through his veins. He launched the dagger again, anyway, relying on its magic to assist in the throw.

The third spider blurred in his vision and the world swam before the Kid's eyes, going watery and his head swooning.

The ground hit him, or at least that's how it seemed.

He lay on his side, panting, but at least Edsumar was back in his hand.

And everything went dark.

The Kid heard concerned voices. They weren't clear, as if he were hearing the conversation underwater.

"I think he's coming to," said a woman.

"It's about time," a deep baritone replied, "I don't believe he was pemtie enough to let those things bite him."

"It's not like we're much better," the woman sounded irritated, "you have at least three broken ribs, and I was knocked unconscious."

"How far do you think the necromancer got?" Torrents asked.

Yes, it was the barbarian, the Kid thought, but wished he hadn't. Thinking, and their talking, made everything spin and lurch.

The Kid rolled to his side and vomited.

"I told you to roll him to his side," Esperanza said.

The Kid felt a gentle touch on his arm, a cool cloth wipe his forehead, then his mouth.

"I'm okay," the Kid tried to say, but it came out as, "Ium oaee."

"What'd he say?" Torrents asked, his voice closer.

"I said," the Kid spoke slowly, his eyes still closed against the spinning, "shut the hell up, hearing hurts right now."

The barbarian laughed, the sound retreating.

The Kid's leg throbbed with each heartbeat, and he panted—his mouth open—wondering if he was going to be sick again.

"Can you drink?" Esperanza asked, the cool cloth still scraping across the Kid's swollen skin.

"Just let me die, dammit," the Kid mumbled into the grass poking into his cheek, and passed out again.

It was dark when the Kid woke. Pushing upright, he let the spinning subside before opening his eyes.

He didn't feel as bad as before. His stomach only lurched from the effort, threatening to let loose again.

The campfire had burned down to glowing coals, and the Kid lay a couple of meters from it.

Probably so I don't roll over into it, the Kid thought.

His leg still throbbed, and he probed at it with one hand. He stopped, realizing he still clutched Edsumar.

Good morning, sleeping beauty, the dagger said silently.

How do you know that movie? The Kid asked in his mind because it was easier than trying to talk with his dry throat and pounding head.

I've had some time to poke around in your head while you were sleeping, Edsumar said cheerfully. *You didn't have your normal defenses up when you were fighting the poison. On the bright side, that also allowed me to gift you with some of the dragon fortitude we're so famous for.*

You went through my head? The Kid wasn't pleased.

Indeed, Edsumar said, *and it's very interesting in here. Lots of stuff you keep hidden away.*

"Hey there," Esperanza knelt beside him, placing a hand on the Kid's shoulder, "how're you feeling?"

It was a testament to how he felt when he realized he hadn't heard her approaching.

"I'm okay," the Kid croaked, and looked at her, then squinted up at the sky, "and what're you doing up, this isn't your watch."

"Well," the priestess handed him an unstoppered canteen, "Torrents needed sleep, he's got a few cracked ribs and the poultice PepperGarten gave us made him sleepy after carrying you here. And you were in no condition to take a watch. In fact, I'm surprised you're awake already. It was a helluva bite, really nasty. I think most people would've died from it."

The Kid drank from the canteen. Then rinsed his mouth out and spit it to one side, then drank again.

"Yeah," the Kid lifted the dagger, "Edsumar said he helped with that."

"Handy guy," Esperanza smiled, "and easy on the water, don't want to upset your tummy again."

"Stow it," the Kid said with no real menace, "I've been taking care of sick people since before your parents were born."

"Maybe," the priestess sat back on her haunches, "and it seems the old adage is true then, doctors make the worst patients."

Meeting her eyes, the Kid searched her face. Sighing, he looked down.

"Thanks," the Kid said, "I really appreciate you guys doing this for me. You saved my life."

"Only after you saved mine," Esperanza observed her reluctant patient, "so we can just call it even and move on."

"Move on?" the Kid rubbed at his head, and realized he still held Edsumar.

He looked around for the sheath he'd carved, and noticed that they'd cut away his pants, removed his belt, and rolled him in a blanket. He waved towards his pack.

"Hand me that, would you?" the Kid said, "Please?"

"Yeah," Esperanza laughed.

Standing and grabbing the bag, she passed it to the Kid. She waited for him to settle back down before talking.

"The necromancer is gone," she said quietly, "heading south as best as we can tell. It's going to be hell catching up with her."

"Can we talk about it in the morning," growled a lump from the other side of the fire, "some of us are trying to sleep."

"So are the poultices alchemical magic?" the Kid asked.

They were walking along an animal track, moving south, through knee-high grass, following the eastern border of the Blue Desert.

Torrents led the way, picking out the easiest path while leaning on his walking staff. His ribs were still painful and healing.

"I think it might be," Esperanza said, "because these things PepperGarten gave us sure don't work like a normal one. They do a lot more. I've seen magical healing, and it can take a bunch of different forms. Some alchemists make potions, others make hot rocks, acupuncture needles, salves, creams, lotions, and once I even saw a gunpowder-like substance that exploded in a fiery flash and left the flesh healed afterwards."

The Kid grunted.

"Where do you think this witch is headed?" the Kid asked.

"You're full of questions today, aren't you?" Esperanza laughed. "And take it easy on the witch thing. You know, some folks might call me the same thing. A weather witch."

"Well, you aren't trying to kill everyone," the Kid quipped, "so I don't think we'll prepare the stake and bonfire for you quite yet."

"Good to hear," the priestess smiled sadly for a moment, then went on, "I think she's headed for the place with the largest population of people. Durgan's Keep."

"Looks like I'm going to get to show you guys my city then," the Kid said.

Chapter 22

The three debated how to best describe the color of the sands of the Blue Desert. They all agreed that the further south they went, the more it reminded them of a blue highlighter. But further to the north, it was a deeper color, but not dark. They settled on agreeing that it was closest to a Wal-Mart blue.

What really made them wonder was the ten-meter-wide white path down the center. Calling upon the power of her goddess, Latress, Esperanza said that the blue sands held a very faint aura of magic, but the white streak was almost the antithesis of magic, and grabbed at her mystical probing and pulled it into the absence of color and magic.

"It wasn't here before," Esperanza said, "this is something new. And considering how wide it is, just about as wide as an undead army marching in rank and formation, I think our friend the necromancer may have had something to do with this."

"What's that even mean?" Torrents asked. "Did she have her undead legion bleaching the sand as they walked, in some weird Mister Miyagi, Karate Kid, lesson sort of thing?"

"I don't think so," the Kid chimed in, "but that'd be hilarious to see!"

"No," Esperanza said, "I think the necromancer was draining the magical runoff from the Nine Towers of Magic to help shore up her own magics and strengthen her army."

They traveled south for more than a week, hampered by their injuries, though they grew healthier each day. After the fourth day, they found the fresh wreckage of a caravan.

Manacles and chains, smeared with dried blood, were strung along behind one wagon, and crates of food were still among the carts.

"I know this group," Torrents said, inspecting the shattered wagons and mutilated horses, and held up a banner showing the silhouette of a wolf's head in front of a red circle. "This is the Blood Sun Wolf slavers. But I don't get it."

The barbarian fell silent, staring at the banner.

The Kid picked through the rubble, looking for a sword to replace the one he'd lost at the Nine Towers.

"Don't get what?" Esperanza toed at the torn form of a chicken.

"Slavers are very proprietary," Torrents explained, still holding the banner in his hand, "and no other slaver clan would use the banner of another. But I saw the caravan master, Dropsum, dead and laying under a bush."

"Notice something missing?" the Kid shouted from the front of the line to the back where the other two were.

Esperanza and Torrents looked around, then the priestess raised her arms in an exaggerated shrug.

"No bodies," the Kid said as he approached his companions, inspecting a saber he'd found. "There are no bodies at all, except for the animals. Who would attack a caravan, kill all the animals, and take the people?"

"Do you think the necromancer attacked these people?" Esperanza asked.

"Nope," the Kid said, rocking from his toes to his heels, "no guards, either. There wasn't a fight here. There are no bodies, no guards, no signs of struggle."

"So," Esperanza looked around, "what's that mean?"

"They were working together," Torrents said quietly. "Dropsum and his Blood Sun Wolf slaver clan were in league with Aku'ji this whole time. That would explain the bodies missing from his caravan the day after I destroyed it. And that probably means the screams in the night were the other slaves being caught and…"

Torrents went quiet, leaving the thought hanging.

"But then that must also mean Dropsum himself is some form of undead," Esperanza said, "maybe one of the higher undead, which have complete free will, free thought, and their own agendas."

"Well then," the Kid said, tossing a horseshoe side-handed and making it skip across the pale blue sands, "I guess that means all the slaves here, and the guards, and anyone who was with this caravan, have now joined Aku'ji undead legion."

"These bastards just keep getting bigger, badder, and better, don't they?" Torrents sighed and turned to the south to walk away from the caravan.

Over the remaining four-day journey south, they found more than one more caravan in the same condition, but each of these showed signs of struggle, though still didn't have any corpses except for mauled and mutilated animals.

They arrived at the small village that served as a port for the Inner Bay, the same village where Captain Jaimin had dropped the Kid off.

It took three more days to contact, then await the arrival of, the Raptor Rex via a carrier pigeon with a small enchantment from the Kid so it would seek out a moving location.

Once they'd set sail, the Captain called them to his cramped quarters. The ceiling was just under two meters high, and Torrents had to bend over to move around the cabin. The tall tables along the walls held maps, the table in the center held whiskey bottles and cups in a recess in the top. A cubby on the side of the room had the captain's bunk with drawers underneath.

The four sat around the table, after sharing a meal, and raised the ceramic cups of whiskey in a toast.

"Here's to each sunrise," Captain Jaimin intoned solemnly, "and hoping we each get a reason for something else to rise, whether it be our spirits, or our cocks!"

The rotund man laughed, and the three others stared at him, unused to such humor.

"Ladies excluded in that," the Captain corrected, still smiling, "for you I'm sure you can find something else that will rise, whether it be your nipples or your ire, and I'd say it be the latter right now."

The bearded man laughed again, looking around at the three somber faces.

"Look, kids," the Captain said, "either you learn to laugh anytime you can, or you die without laughing, because that second part is a certainty."

"Then here's to nipples and cocks," the Kid said, raising his cup again, "and may they be harder than every day we face."

The four toasted, clinking the drinking vessels and threw back their individual mouthfuls of whiskey.

"Now," the Kid said, "can we discuss a plan? Can you tell us where the undead horde is now?"

"Yeah," Jaiman said, "I can, and I will, and none of you'll like it. Those rotten rotters are at the gates of Durgan's Keep. They've been there for almost two days, from what the news that the doves bring me says."

"You talk to doves?" Esperanza leaned forward in interest.

"No, no, no, my dear," Jaimin laughed, "I have doves show up with little notes attached to their legs."

"Oh," Esperanza looked disappointed.

"Then the birds talk to me and tell me what the note says," the man said with a wide grin, "but I don't talk to them, that'd be silly!"

The priestess eyed the man, unsure if he was serious or joking.

"Durgan's Keep," the Kid reminded, "what else can you tell us?"

"Well," Jaimin continued. "Aku'ji—and she does like the sound of her own voice, doesn't she, been shouting out her name and titles every chance she gets—but as I was saying, Aku'ji has been scooping every farmer, merchant, and villager within the area around Durgan's Keep, and her forces keep growing. Even the camp followers who'd normally trail after a group like that—repairing armor and cooking pots, or even ladies of the night who sell their services to lonely men—they've all been scooped up and absorbed in one way or another, either as a meal for the more powerful undead who need such things, or as one more foot soldier damned to serve beyond death. Not to mention any of the city guard and militia that's slain in battle. It's only a matter of time before she either gets in or has made every living soul in the city into one of her minions."

"And our side?" the Kid asked. "How're they holding up? Any routes in or out? Any real resistance to speak of that might help us?"

"Wait," Jaimin held up a finger, "you want to go there?"

"Yes," Esperanza said quickly, "of course we do. Why else would we have contacted you?"

"My good looks and charm leap to mind," the Captain said with a guffaw, "but I'm glad to hear it. Looks like we have some heroes in the making. Either that, or we have three more undead warriors looking for a line to be conscripted. Let's hope it's the former, eh?"

The room grew quiet, and the three companions exchanged looks.

Torrents opened his mouth to say something, but the Captain interrupted him.

"Look, kids," Jaiman poured another round of drinks, "you got this, okay? I have faith in you, and it's better than running, right? Here's what I know that'll help: Captain Mezk has been building a resistance, shipping women and children out over the bay, and bringing in troops."

"Wait," the Kid held up a hand. "Mezk? Mezk the Damned? The one who made the deal with the demons?"

Jaimin nodded, then threw back his drink. He looked back to the Kid with a gasp from the burn of the drink and squinted.

"Don't you think he might have his own agenda attached to some things that are just as bad," the Kid continued, "if not worse than the necromancer?"

"The enemy of my enemy is my friend," the Captain said, "at least until that first enemy is gone and my once friend is back to being my enemy and stabbing my face."

Torrents tossed back his drink in response and Esperanza followed his example.

The priestess fingered her small knife, wondering if the time to use it was overdue, if she should've ended this long before now. But she had to help if she could.

"But Mezk can get you into the city," the Captain said, "which is currently surrounded by the thousands of undead. That, in itself, will be a feat of legend. And if you guys come out on top in this one, I'll buy you each a bottle of my favorite rotgut. Which is extremely cheap, so this isn't a really big kindness."

A knock on the door made them all turn and look.

"Come," Captain Jaimin shouted towards the door.

A mop top of red hair leaned in. It was Jundek, the sailor the Kid remembered from his first trip on this ship.

"Captain," Jundek, not much more than just a boy, said, "you'd better come see this, and bring them, too."

They filed onto the deck. To the south, the evening was a bright orange with a black layer above it, looking like a bad impersonation of the actual setting sun in the west.

On the shore, just a league away, Durgan's Keep was burning.

Chapter 23

Two hours later Torrents, Esperanza, and the Kid crouched in a rowboat, a black tarp covering them, with a magical breeze from the enchanted tiller pushing them gently towards shore.

Mezk the Damned steered the boat, the two sailors—Jundek and Tillheim—ready on each side with padded oars to help if needed. A knit cap covered Mezk's carrot-orange hair, and he'd bent his lean, lanky form almost double under the canvas covering above them.

"You think you'd work a different hair color into your deal with the demons," the Kid muttered.

"Shut it," Mezk growled, "sound carries on the water, and these things around Durgan's Keep don't need much encouragement to swarm us and drag us down to the depths."

The immense wall, about fifty meters tall—which the Kid had explained earlier was about the height of a fifteen or eighteen story building, depending when it was built—rose into the darkness above them. The orange glow of fires danced across the face of buildings above, showing the city had been penetrated and the invaders were now inside.

The city had been designed for different purposes on many different levels. It had warrens underneath, dug into the bedrock behind the cliff, which had been designed and excavated by the rokairn. It had a wooded aeifain and dasism section with gardens and trees. It had a housing quarter, a marketplace and merchant quarter, an administration section, and other smaller areas, and each could be closed off from the others for defensive purposes.

There was a chance that the whole was taken, but only some contained the attackers, but they wouldn't know until they got there.

"There," Mezk pointed halfway up the rock face, "we're going through a sewer opening there. We'll need to move through the docks, and up the switchbacks until we get high enough. Then we scale the cliff side, unlock and open the bars covering the sewers, and enter them. Once inside, we can go about anywhere, depending if these damned things are in the tunnels or not."

The boat scraped something, rocking gently. They slowed, and Mezk stared at the bottom of the boat with concern.

"Did we hit something?" Esperanza whispered. "A submerged tree branch, maybe? I mean, this bay is too deep for that to be the bottom this far out, right?"

"Hush," Mezk breathed, turning his head to listen for the sound of anything touching the bottom of their craft.

Something scratched at the bottom, a long thin noise with the hiccupping pop of whatever skipping in the divots of wood on the bottom of the boat.

The craft rocked again, this time more violently.

"That's not a tree," Torrents said, pulling a long dagger from the sheath on his waist.

The two men, Jundek and Tillheim, accompanying Mezk, tensed and looked at one another, fear in their eyes. They drew dirks with soot blackened blades in one hand, and a hatchet in their other.

Mezk increased their speed, moving closer to the docks ahead. The wharf held no boats or ships, having been abandoned when the undead creatures had surrounded the city, including patrolling along the walls, around the area, and under the water.

The bay side held no lights, and no moon shone tonight, so the area was dark except for the occasional flaming brand that fell from above.

The boat thunked into something, and a grizzled hand appeared on the bow, rocking the small craft further. A second hand appeared next to the first, and then a third, a fourth, and a fifth. A withered face rose above the side, as something lifted itself from the water and tried to pull itself aboard.

Torrents slashed at the face with his blade, cutting across the thing's cheeks and the bridge of its nose. It continued to drag itself up.

"No," said Tillheim, "when the enemy is boarding, you cut his ties."

As the man said this in a whisper, he brought down his hatchet twice, once on each hand of the creature, with a ka-chunk, and severed the fingers.

The thing slid back into the water.

Jundek was duplicating the actions on the other side of the rowboat as two more of the things crested the bow.

Torrents imitated them on another undead when it rose in front of him, and the Kid joined.

The tarp that had covered them had been folded back, and now the breeze caught at it and tugged it further. The things pulling themselves up, scrambled at the tarp, using it as a line to gain access to the men inside the boat.

Mezk drew his thin blade and began slicing the rope that threaded itself through the eyelets of the tarp to hold it over the rowboat. The canvas slid away, dragged by the weight of a half dozen waterlogged creatures.

They did this as silently as possible, not wanting to draw any more attention than they already had. The loudest noise was the dull thump of a hatchet cutting through bone and sinew. Soon, they pulled away from the creatures, leaving many of them with no hands.

Within minutes, they bumped against the docks, the two sailors dropping pads over the side to soften the noise; and using their wrapped oars to guide them to the plank walkway with as little sound as possible.

Mezk tied off his craft while the others clambered onto the wharf. Then he followed, taking up the rear of the line.

Jundek led the way towards the stone walkway, as wide as three wagons, that wound its way up the cliff side, doubling back and forth and towards their destination.

When they'd reached the first switchback, wet sounds floated through the darkness from the where they'd tied off the boat. The slap of waterlogged feet sounded from below them, as the creatures from the depths followed their path.

Jundek, in the lead, moved faster, but was limited in how fast he could move because of the lack of light. If they lit a torch or lantern, it would be a beacon for the undead, and soon they would be overwhelmed.

A figure landed in front of them, crumpling to the ground with the sound of breaking bones and splattering flesh. A second followed, but this one continued to move once it had shattered on the stone, and reached up towards Esperanza with a twisted claw.

Torrents interceded between the two, and with a shove of his booted foot, the broken body flew off the side of the walkway and to the boardwalk below.

Something landed gently behind him, and claws raked down his spine, hampered by his thick cloak.

The Kid, with his vision enhanced to see in the dark from the ability bestowed upon him by Edsumar, saw the lank, dark form drop from above and land in front of him. The thing attacked Torrents, ignoring everyone else.

The Kid stabbed upward, aiming for the base of the creature's skull. His blade slid into the brain, catching slightly on a vertebra, and bumping sideways so the point jutted out of an eye socket.

Three more forms fell in quick succession, each creature dropping into a crouch and hissing, long claws flexing.

The Kid remembered these things surrounding the newly made zombies and feeding on them to increase their own resilience and power. They also matched the description that Torrents had given of the thing he'd faced in the Black Wood with Axle, before he arrived in Hope's Hollow.

Two of the things leapt at Tillheim in the middle of the group, bringing him down like wolves picking out a deer from the herd. One ripped out the man's throat in a spray of blood, and the others tore into the man's gut with both hands, disemboweling him. A quiet gurgle rose from the sailor as he tried to scream, falling under their assault.

It also cut the group in half, with the Kid and Mezk on one side of the monsters, and Torrents, Esperanza, and the remaining sailor on the other.

A whispered prayer from Esperanza drifted on the wind, which then rose and became a mist that wrapped itself around the things, glowing with a gentle light that wouldn't be seen more than a meter away.

Mezk shoved the Kid aside, knocking him to the ground, and spun into action. His own black blade gleamed with a red glow as he sliced into the creatures. They fell under his onslaught, wisps of red energy drifting from their crumbling forms, and were sucked into the weapon in the carrot-top's hand. The two undead figures were dust before they hit the ground.

Edsumar growled in the Kid's head.

Torrents made quick work of the third creature, who now stood, wobbling, with no head on top of its shoulders. It took three steps forward, its hands flailing for a foe, stumbling, collapsed to the ground. It tipped over the edge of the walkway and fell into the darkness below.

Moving around the broken bodies, and leaving the fallen Tillheim behind, the group moved forward, once again in darkness.

The Kid, able to see, didn't miss Mezk leaning down to stab each body—including his own man—as he moved past them, his dirk draining them of their life, or death, force.

"Here," Mezk said after they had moved up a couple more switchbacks, "it's to our right, and we're going to need to scale the cliff face."

"In the dark?" Esperanza's voice quavered.

"Hold on," Mezk said, his voice even and patient.

The thin man leaned down and rolled something along the thin path to their right. A rope lit up with a dull red throb, a ball of light every two meters. The magical hemp hugged the corner of the walkway against the wall.

The path itself was about the width of two men abreast, which would normally be ample room for anyone to walk comfortably. But the added drop off, with jagged rocks, undead soldiers, and black water below, made it feel like it was much thinner than anyone cared to admit.

Mezk took the lead, walking with ease down the trail, the Kid close behind him.

The Kid was sticking close to Mezk quite on purpose.

As the Godfather once said, 'Keep your friends close, and your enemies closer,' the Kid thought, *and besides, I want to see what other tricks this guy had picked up from his demon buddies. Not everyone had a soul stealing dagger and nightlight rope in their back pocket.*

The Kid also wondered if anyone could use those things, or if there were strings attached and bad things would come if used. He figured it was better to not risk it.

Mezk reached the sewer gate. It was an archway, about a meter wide, and a meter and a half tall, with an iron gate across it. The lock on the hasp, holding it closed from the inside, looked new.

Arrayed behind the Kid on the walkway were Esperanza, Torrents, and then Jundek. Esperanza hugged the wall, facing it, and panting shallowly. Torrents had one hand between her shoulder blades, perhaps to comfort her, perhaps to keep her from falling over the side, but most likely it was a bit of both.

The gate swung outward into the open air with a high-pitched squeal, and Mezk jumped on it, holding a hand out to assist everyone in getting into the sewer without mishap.

The Kid easily leapt across the space, ignoring the proffered hand, landing cat-like inside and moving forward so the next person could get in.

Esperanza took Mezk's hand, and then grabbed his entire arm, jerking him off balance when she pulled him to her. Mezk wrapped his arm around her torso as Torrents lifted her towards the opening. The gate swung, assisted by Torrents's long reach, and Esperanza was safely deposited inside the tunnel. She rushed forward to the Kid, grabbing at him, panting, and looked away from the opening and the threatening drop that could have led to her death.

Torrents made the transfer easily, followed by the sailor, and then Mezk joined them.

The thin man swung the gate closed—catching it with one hand to make minimal noise—carefully replaced the lock, and clipped it shut. Pulling on the glowing rope with a specific sequence of movements, Mezk reeled it in as the light faded from the magical hemp.

Their guide gestured them forward into the darkness.

"Keep a hand on the right-side wall," Mezk whispered, barely audible, "and when we get to the first intersection, we can use a light."

They moved forward, their feet sloshing through the thick liquid. The smell of waste, human and otherwise, filled their noses. Things squished and wiggled past their feet, and the occasional sound of rushing water echoed through the tunnel. Each time the sound died down to a trickle, and moments later they'd feel a wash of warmer liquid move past their boots.

"Okay," Jundek said, "we're here. You can light a lantern now."

Soft squelching noises came from the sailor as he shuffled his feet and waited.

Esperanza fumbled with her satchel, not wanting to set it in down in the sewers, until she found what she needed. Holding the lantern aloft, she called upon a miniscule trickle of power from her goddess, and an electric spark jumped from her fingers to light the wick of her lantern.

Light flared.

Raising the lantern above her head, she turned to survey the intersection in front of the sailor.

The squelching noises still came from Jundek; held aloft, his throat torn, a half dozen undead creatures fed on his twitching body.

Chapter 24

The undead creatures looked up, their sunken eyes shifting in their sockets. These weren't the common low undead that the majority of the army consisted of, neither were these like the ones they had faced on the path up from the docks. These seemed much more wild, not mindless, just feral.

Their jaws dropped, unhinging, until the mandible stretched their skin unnaturally and hung to their collar bones. A screeching sound echoed through the tunnels from the unnatural horrors, causing the Kid to throw his hands over his ears.

The things launched themselves towards the remaining four warm bodies, dropping the still twitching sailor.

Torrents caught one by the throat and crushed its windpipe. Reaching up with the other hand, the huge barbarian twisted the neck—reminding him of opening a pickle jar back home. Just a little muscle and twist would do it—and tore the head from the body. A thick liquid, which wasn't quite blood and burned his skin, sprayed across him.

Mezk whirled into motion, spinning through the gathering of undead, striking with his dagger. Two of the creatures, drained of their essence, disintegrated. Dust filtered down to the wet floor of the sewer.

The Kid threw his dagger. The ivory blade pierced a creature's eye, who fell into the runoff with a splash.

The two remaining creatures focused on Esperanza, drawn by the mystical connection between her and Latress.

Esperanza, unfocused after the heights, stumbled backwards and screamed. Lightning shot from her fingertips—reminding Torrents of Emperor Palpatine from Star Wars. The attackers melted into twisted, smoking husks of tight, black flesh and bones, and fell to the ground.

Mezk stabbed each form, dead or undead, with his dagger. Unabashed by the others watching the interaction, he drew in a deep breath as the weapon drew in the energy from within the being.

He smiled at Esperanza—who stared at the man, horrified after seeing the ritual for the first time—and winked at the Kid, who watched him through slitted eyes.

Why would anyone create beings such as this? Esperanza thought, as the group, down to four, moved forward. *Nature wouldn't do this, and I don't know why any god would allow this. Does that mean these are of man's creation?*

The four of them moved through the sewers, facing down groups of the undead invaders, and destroying them. It disturbed each of the companions whenever Mezk pulled the soul from a fallen foe, but they needed him, so kept their thoughts to themselves.

Led by the Kid, within an hour of entering the subterranean tunnels, they found their way to an exit near the red-light district along the docks.

Around them, the city burned.

The thick smoke roiled above the parapets and walkways of the city watch. Groups of militia or the different street guilds moved past in clumps, eyes wary and searching for the lurching and shambling forms of the enemy.

Clouds gathered overhead, reflecting the light of the fires within the city walls, casting shadows into the alleys and streets.

Women and children screamed when an undead squad found them, attacked them, tore them limb from limb, devouring them in the middle of the street. Men shouted to one another, trying to come together to create a force that could defend the city, one of the last standing bastions against the demonic hordes in the south.

The group realized that most of the fires had been set by the citizens to hamper or kill the undead army, but it had also created events and situations that just as easily killed civilians.

Chaos reigned.

The Kid scaled a wall, climbing it without effort, his fingers finding nooks and crannies without trying, and ran along the top, looking out across the burning city. He called down to the others, letting them know when they approached a group of the enemy, allowing them to avoid the encounter altogether.

They moved through the city, facing enemies when they had to, and moving towards the Kid's goal, the red-light district.

Mezk bristled at being under the Kid's guidance, unhappy about how the Kid made him the fool, along with an entire crew of Bokk's men. Mezk had no boss, but freelanced with any side that would sign a contract and keep their word. More than one person who'd broken a contract with the demon damned mercenary had been found dead afterwards.

In just under a half hour, the Kid led them to the whoring part of town, and to Jewlnee in particular. The building differed from just a few weeks before.

Iron banded shutters, painted in yellows, pinks, and reds, battened and latched across every door and window. Only the cross shape of the arrow slits showed evidence of people within, and the point of a bolt balanced on a crossbow always accompanied it.

The Kid knew Jewlnee's routine, and two women would be behind any one woman holding the weapon. One would wait to reload the crossbow, and the second was there to pass a loaded weapon to the person staffing the arrow slit, or to replace them if they fell.

With a word and twist of his wrist, Mezk sent his rope up the side of the building, and it wound itself around the spindles in the balcony above, and then knotted itself along its own length to make the climb quicker and easier for those below.

Mezk leapt from the ground to the veranda without effort, but Torrents and Esperanza used the rope.

The Kid leapt from the adjacent building to join the others. Standing with his back to the wall, the Kid knocked on the shutter.

"Hey," the Kid called as the crossbow point pivoted in his direction, "who's in there? Go get Jewlnee for me."

"And who the hell are you?" a young woman's voice answered.

"I'm the Kid," the Kid replied, realizing he only had one name, like Madonna, or Cher, or…he couldn't think of any men that just went by a solo moniker.

"The Kid," the voice grew flustered, "as in, THE Kid? Are you as cute as they say?"

"Oh, by Latress's blustery locks," Esperanza sighed, and then banged on the shutter with her fist, "go get the damned madam and quit your swooning before we all chuzzing die out here. That's the words of Esperanza, priestess of Latress, and destroyer of disease, okay already?"

A squeak came from inside, and they could hear retreating footfalls. Two other young, giggling voices came from inside.

Within a few minutes, the painted and effervescent Jewlnee arrived, opened the shutters, and welcomed the Kid and his friends inside, though she gave a second look and consideration to Mezk. They allowed him in only after the Kid reassured Jewlnee he was on their side and helping.

Shortly after entering, the five of them sat around a table, grapes, cheese, bread, and wine set out in the center. They raised their glasses in a toast, though Mezk looked like an animal that wanted open air rather than being trapped inside.

"To freedom," Jewlnee said, "though most people never realize they have it, don't have it, or the cost of having it."

They raised their glasses, clinking every other glass before drinking to avoid the bad luck of missing one.

After a deep drink, they talked.

"Jewlnee," the Kid said, "I came right to you because I knew you'd have your ear to the ground, and your finger on the pulse of the city. Can you help us find Aku'ji, the necromancer?"

"You're going after her?" Jewlnee asked with a gasp, then laughed, "I should've known you would.

You never knew when to quit, and since I last saw you, you seem even more driven, even a little crazy, but with purpose. Like it isn't the same young man I've known for years. Who's in that head now, Kid?"

"Let's just say," the Kid gave the madam a crooked smile, "I'm an old soul, and then a little more on top of that. Can you help us?"

"Yes," the woman said hesitantly, "but she has layers of defense, and she's already calling out for allies within Durgan's Keep. Asking for those that want to survive this occupation to come forward and give her intelligence."

"You mean," the Kid sneered, popping a grape into his mouth, "turn others in."

"Yeah," Jewlnee agreed, "toss them to the wolves. And these people think that they'll come out on top, and when this is all said and done, they'll be holding the cards and have some iota of control within Durgan's Keep."

"Tell us about these layers of defense," Esperanza urged.

"And do some name dropping on these allies, if you would please," said Torrents.

The meeting took hours to play out, Jewlnee calling for maps and informants hidden in the basement below. Between the hours before and after midnight, she brought sausages, hot teas, and other things to keep the group moving and awake. By midmorning, the witching hour, each person was heading out in a different direction with a different task.

Each knew they may not see the others again and were prepared for that.

At the moment of parting, Mezk slipped away from the others without a word, and the three friends that had been through so much together faced one another.

"Be careful out there, Kid," Esperanza smiled at the young man, then turned to Torrents, "you might be a big bad ass, but don't push your luck, a dagger in your ribs kills you as much as anyone."

"Whatever," the barbarian muttered, "your face kills you as much as anyone."

They chuckled together, not because of the humor, but to share the moment.

"Yeah," the Kid sighed, "you kids take of yourself, and I want to hear that call soon, okay Esperanza? You find that bitch, and then you call us to you. We'll answer, if we can."

"Kid?" Torrents said, turning towards the smaller man.

"Yeah, big guy?" The Kid looked up at the barbarian.

Torrents enveloped the Kid in a hug, and pulled the street thief to his chest, holding him close for a few moments.

"You'd have been a great grandma to have," Torrents said as he released the Kid.

"And you're a bidj and pemtie," the Kid's voice was rough as he grabbed the big man's biceps and stared into the other's eyes, "now, go kick some bidj, you big dummy, and let's save the city."

The three moved apart, taking one last glance at the spot they'd stood a moment before, and at one another, and then turned away and moved into the night.

Torrents sought the merchant district, hunting the slave master, Dropsum.

The Kid had learned that Jakdin had switched sides, and his big plan for the city was to throw all the other guild masters under the bus by aligning with the necromancer, and then ruling the underworld once his competition was dead. The Kid hunted Jakdin.

Esperanza called upon her goddess as she moved away from the others, asking for her blessing and guidance in finding the source of the evil in the city.

Chapter 25

Torrents moved through the streets, staying on the walls and avoiding the center of any avenue. He wasn't a master tactician, but he had enough sense to know that taking out the army one at a time would be the path to a quick death.

To turn this one into a win, they had to take out the head of the snake. And to do that, they needed to cut the legs out from under the snake.

Torrents, ducking behind an overturned cart to avoid being spotted by a squad of undead patrolling the area, realized that snakes didn't have legs, but he knew what he meant.

Moving along the outer wall to the Merchant Quarter, the barbarian crouched in the shadows when he could see the stone archway that led to the shops and businesses. It was guarded, sort of. It had four undead on each side of the opening, and Torrents could see four more on both sides within the entrance.

That made sixteen shambling, lurching, shuffling, mildly dazed, and barely cognizant people lumbering back and forth. The things meandered back and forth, one bumping into a wall, another picking at a lump of moss on a cobblestone, and the others equally engaged and vigilant.

Torrents still didn't think going straight down the middle was the answer. Time to take a page from the Kid's book.

Moving down the street a little, until the archway was out of sight, blocked by buildings, the barbarian looked around to make sure no one was watching or approaching.

He slid his sword into the scabbard on his back, bent at the knees, jumped up, and grabbed the overhang of the porch of a cobbler's shop. Pulling himself up, he moved along the shingled surface, taking his time so he didn't make noise and attract unwanted attention.

The building was built flush to the inner-city wall, and Torrents moved across the roof to the thin parapet behind the shop. Vaulting over it, he landed on another roof. He crept to the edge and looked down into the street.

That's when an idea struck him.

If he could drop the portcullis at each of the entrances to the Merchant Quarters, then it would probably stop most of the undead from getting out, or more from coming in.

This was a genius idea! These things weren't really bright enough to figure how to raise the gate once he'd dropped it, and Torrents didn't see anyone hanging out that looked like they were in charge and could give orders or instructions for such a task.

The barbarian turned back and moved to the parapet he'd crossed, mounted it, and moved along it—bent over and keeping low to remain unseen—towards the archway.

When he came to it, he wondered if he knew enough about such things to drop the gate. He'd seen movies, but was unsure how realistic they'd been. And even if they were historically accurate, it didn't mean that this world would have developed the same technology in the same way.

Scrambling atop the stone crossover, which was about five meters across, he saw the wooden trapdoors in the roof. He opened one, slowly, to keep any noises to a minimum, and saw iron rungs that led down to the small guardroom. And wow, it was small, barely big enough for one man to turn around in. But within it was a wheel with a crank, and it held the chain with a chock to keep the portcullis up.

Moving down the metal ladder, he saw the things outside the small room, wandering back and forth. Two of the undead were nose to nose, trying to go around one another. Each moved in the same direction, mirroring one another as they tried to pass the other.

Torrents watched them move back and forth for almost a full minute before dropping one leg down, and placing his booted foot on the lever that held the chain in place. He extended his leg, moving the lever, and with a series of loud clicks, the chain disengaged, and the portcullis dropped.

The two zombie-like creatures were still moving side to side, trying to go past one another. The outside one was crushed, metal spikes on the bottom of the gate piercing his skull and driving him to the cobblestones. The second looked down, tilted his head at his crushed counterpart, sighed, turned around, and walked to the second portcullis that had dropped into place. Seeing his return way blocked, he turned again, walked back to where the other one had been impaled, sighed, and turned back again. This seemed to be this thing's destiny, as it repeated the actions again and again.

Torrents climbed out of the trapdoor above and moved along the wall to the next guard post for the Merchant's Quarter. He repeated his actions at each of the remaining four entries, then dropped over the wall into the marketplace.

Moving past the tents and stalls, and through the slave market, he made his way towards the Merchant's Guild, where they had thought was the best chance of finding Dropsum.

Seeing the building ahead, Torrents crouched and studied the surrounding movement.

People in chains lined the road outside, and dark, gaunt, humanoid creatures walked along, poking and hissing at them. The prisoners jerked away from the things, trying to stay out of their reach, but unable to do so because of their shackles.

The lead captive, the one closest to the door of the building, had been unchained and was being dragged inside as three other citizens came trudging out. The three leaving were following another undead, who hit their freshly dead and animated flesh with a riding crop, guiding them to a makeshift corral where others like them stood dumbly waiting.

Torrents needed inside, and he needed to get there without having to fight a horde of the things standing guard over the prisoners. He needed a distraction. But he also wanted to free the people.

He needed a plan.

Well, the barbarian thought, *squatting in an alley isn't going to free the people, get the guards away from the door, or get me inside. I need to do something.*

Torrents doubled back, giving a wide berth, then crossed the road and crept along the buildings towards the line of captives.

He'd moved past a handful of them before the first one noticed him in the shadows. The woman let out gasp, staring at him. He held his finger to his lips to silence her, moving to the ring set into the stone of the ground to which the prisoners were chained.

Squatting over it and gripping it, he pushed up with his legs. The muscles in his shoulders, arms, back, and legs bunched with the effort.

The woman, seeing what he was doing, turned to the people next to her and whispered something. In almost perfect unison, the prisoners began wailing, shouting, and rattling their chains, clumping together to block out the sight and sound of what was happening behind them.

"Make some noise," a man shouted, "they can chain our bodies, but they can't chain our spirits!"

The line of prisoners came to life, some hesitating and looking around in a daze, but others causing the distraction that the barbarian needed.

The ring tore from the ground. Torrents dropped it, nodded at the captives looking back at him, and moved to the next ring.

The creatures guarding the people beat them with short whips, clubs, and crops, hissing between the cracks of leather hitting flesh.

The second ring freed, Torrents moved to the third and final one.

One guard shouted, a screeching guttural noise, and pointed directly at the barbarian crouching over the last ring.

Other guards turned to look.

The crowd went wild, surging forward over their captors. Torrents pulled, straining to tear the last obstacle free.

He'd expected the people to flee, but they were in a frenzy, falling onto the monsters that held them captive, ripping them apart with their bare hands. Others snatched up fallen weapons, pieces of wood or metal, and joined in.

Five more creatures rushed out of the building to help quell the uprising.

Torrents slipped behind the chaos, through the open double doors, and into the building.

Moving through the foyer, past the benches along the side of the entryway, and around the wall in front of him, he went to the left instead of right. He realized both directions led to the same large, round room as he entered it.

The room was lit with dozens of oil lanterns, showing most of the tables pushed against the outer wall. Two tables had been pulled together in the center of the chamber, and a person lay manacled to its surface.

Dropsum, the slave trader of the Blood Sun Wolf clan, hunched over the person, holding a black orb that glowed with a deep green inner light, chanting.

Torrents crept forward on cat's feet, drawing his two-handed sword from over his shoulder. Raising it above his head, he swung it down towards Dropsum's shoulder where it met the neck.

The man leaning over the table pivoted and threw his hand up, catching the blade and jerking it from the barbarian's grip.

Smirking, the slave master took a step forward and bashed the handle into the warrior's nose.

Blood spurted, and Torrents stumbled backwards, his hands flying to his face.

Dropsum reversed his grip, holding the blade with both hands, and chopped at his attacker with the crossbar.

Torrents backpedaled, tripping over detritus on the floor, and falling to his butt.

"You again," Dropsum said smoothly, smiling, "you've been a thorn in my side long enough. I think it's time to end this and bring you into the fold. Yes, I think you'll make an excellent lieutenant in my little plan."

Torrents grunted, pulling a broken chair leg from underneath him and throwing it at the man. The projectile hit the man in the face, piercing his eye and jutting out. Black blood dribbled from the wound.

"Chuz you," the barbarian said, "you talk too much."

The slave master screamed, reminiscent of the time Torrents had put an arrow through the man's hand, and swung the pommel of the sword at the barbarian's head.

It was the warrior's turn to catch the weapon, and he pulled it with him when he rolled backwards. The sword slid along Dropsum's palms, cutting them to the bone as it came free.

From his back, Torrents kicked out with both feet as the slave master stumbled forward, and bones cracked, the boots crushing the man's chest.

Dropsum sprawled backwards, hitting the table with the small of his back.

Torrents was on his feet in a flash, thrusting the blade in his enemies' guts, then jerking to one side, tearing the flesh, and causing entrails to spill across the floor.

Dropsum pushed off the table and to his feet, meeting the next blow from the barbarian with his hands, which slid off because of the ichor oozing from the cuts in his palm.

Torrents pummeled at the man, cutting and stabbing with his blade. Dropsum kept coming, wounds closing of their own accord.

The slave master swooned, holding his belly, and smiled up at the barbarian.

"You can't kill me," Dropsum laughed, "I can no longer die, can't you see that?"

Torrents looked around the room, searching for some way to bring the final death of the creature in front of him.

His eyes fell on the black orb on the table.

Dropsum followed his gaze, and his smile faltered.

"No," Dropsum growled, "you won't get out of this that easily."

The slave master threw himself at the magical artifact, covering it with his body, as the barbarian thrust at it with his sword.

The weapon slid into the slave master's back, and Dropsum's form muted the tinkling of breaking glass.

Pulling his blade free, Torrents raised it to strike again, and the slave master rolled to face him.

Shards of the artifact littered the man's midsection, jagged pieces of glass sticking out from ripped flesh and torn organs.

Dropsum's eyes were wide as he looked down at his ruined body, green arcs of magic dancing through his belly. The verdant magic swirled, becoming a thick cloud, and enveloped the slave master. It grew outward into a glowing sphere around the man.

The table beneath the man melted.

Torrents took a step back as the magical forces grew, then turned and ran, skidding around the partition wall between him and the outside.

Reaching the foyer, Torrents paused; the building behind him thrummed, and then exploded, throwing the barbarian a dozen meters into the night air.

The barbarian hit the ground, knocking the air out of him.

Rolling onto his back, Torrents raised his sword to ward off any attacks from the creatures waiting outside, as broken shards of wood and chunks of stone rained down around him.

The courtyard was mostly empty. Many of the prisoners and all undead slavers had disappeared into the night. The remaining captives wandered about, making sure nothing moved that wasn't human, and helping the injured.

The big man called out to the remaining townsfolk.

"Hey," he shouted, then quieted to a harsh whisper, "come with me, we have more work to do to free your city."

People began moving towards him, nodding and gathering fallen weapons to arm themselves.

I found her. Esperanza's voice whispered on the wind. *Follow my words and come to me. Let us end this.*

Chapter 26

The Kid smiled as the body crumpled to the ground. He cleaned the viscous black liquid on the tattered remnants of the undead guard at his feet.

He looked up at the urchins crowded in the corner of the ally and nodded at them, then jerked his head to one side, showing that they should run.

The Kid was on the hunt.

This was never his bag, he was more of the trick them and take it type, running scams on the street, or elaborate heists of the corrupt ruling class here in Durgan's Keep. His skill set, between his innate magics and learned abilities, leaned towards stealth rather than wet work.

He was deep into guild territory now, but couldn't pass by as people were being slaughtered by monsters that he felt partially responsible for. The Kid didn't create them, but he was there when a lot of them were being made into the things that now stalked the streets of his city.

He knew where Jakdin's bolt hole was and had already checked there. The man hadn't been in residence, but a quick interrogation of the man's compatriots had told the Kid where to find the thug he sought.

The people the Kid had found hiding at Jakdin's place weren't the same ones whom he'd tricked that night in the Open Door, but others who now hid from the invading army of the dead; they'd been quick to give up the goods on their boss. They'd confirmed what the Kid had already known: Jakdin was in league with the necromancer, and happy to turn on the thieves of the city, causing them to be turned into new undead.

The Kid made his way back to the rooftops, his own private highway. He moved across the buildings where most people would have normally been sleeping, but with the events of the past few days, most had abandoned their homes, hoping to survive, to see another day.

The growing number of walking dead below told the Kid that most of them had failed.

The Kid's mind magic allowed him to do many things, most of them relating to tricking other people into seeing what he wanted them to see, or not see. These abilities didn't seem to work on the dead masses in the street below. But he still dropped his mental blanket over himself, which made most people not even realize he was there.

Making his way through the city, the Kid arrived in the poor section, called the Cheaps. They were so named for the obvious reasons, but also it was the best place in the city to get someone to sing like a bird for just a few coins, or even just a meal or a bottle of crap booze.

Jakdin had set up his base of operations here.

Dropping into a small courtyard in a circle of apartments, the Kid stood up and surveyed his surroundings, using the night vision given to him by Edsumar.

The buildings rose three stories up on each side of him, most doorways covered by a blanket as much as they were an actual door. The place was as quiet as, well, as quiet as a graveyard. Some buildings still smoldered with fires that had been put out or just burned out, and the smell of scorched wood hung thick in the air. There weren't even rats scurrying about like they normally would be at this hour.

The Kid moved towards a doorway, stopping as footfalls echoed behind him. Wrapping himself in anonymity, he stepped into the shadows beside the door he was about to enter and waited.

Three men entered the courtyard from a doorway across from the Kid, and he recognized them as part of the Grey Ash gang, the people who Jakdin worked with.

"I don't believe this," a weasel faced man said, scratching at his neck vigorously. "This whole thing gives me the willies. I mean, we're feeding these things the people who supported us."

"You mean," the bald man with a limp interjected, holding a lantern up to light their way, "people we used to rob."

"Tomato, tomato," weasel face said, and spat on the ground, "they might be the sheep we fleeced, but they were our people."

"Yeah," the third guy, an immense man with stringy, greasy hair, agreed.

"I just don't think it's right," weasel face whined, "we need them, don't we? We shouldn't be giving them to this witch to make things that would eat our faces as soon as look at us, should we?"

"No," baldy agreed, "but what're we supposed to do? It's not like we can beat them, and Jakdin says he's got it under control. We're not gonna be killed or ate, he said so."

"Yeah," the big guy agreed.

"For now," Weasel whined, "but what about tomorrow, or next week? When does good ol' Jakdin turn on us?"

"Yeah," the big guy added sagely.

"Nothing we can do about it," the bald man sighed, and the three entered another doorway, "but we'd best get him these papers before he decides that today is that day."

"Yeah," echoed the voice of the big man, the three disappearing into the hallway.

The Kid slid from the shadows, moving with barely a noise, and followed the receding light and the sound of the men's voices.

The men continued to complain, though now they talked about the lack of whores in town since the undead army showed up.

The Kid shadowed them through a ramshackle apartment, out into another courtyard, and then they descended a set of stairs into a cellar.

The Kid waited for a count of thirty, giving them time to get ahead and out of sight, then entered the basement.

He heard the men debating if the undead would take the place of people in the city, doing the tasks they'd need, when the deep baritone of the big man hushed them. One man knocked on a door, and a muffled voice shouted something. The sound of it closing followed the creaking of the rusty hinges of a door, and the voices became muted.

Oh great, the Kid thought, *how am I supposed to get into a closed room without being noticed?*

You could wait until they come out, Edsumar suggested in the Kid's head.

The Kid moved to the door, pressed his ear to it, and listened.

The thick wood stopped him from making out the words, but he could hear four voices. He recognized Jakdin's sneer as the man harangued the three who'd just entered. It sounded like it was coming from an antechamber.

The Kid risked it. Crouching low and cloaking himself in his magics, he pulled down on the lever and opened the door a few centimeters.

Looking into the room, he couldn't see anyone in the lamplight that filled the area.

Taking a deep breath, he pushed the door open wide enough to slip inside, duck walked in, turning as he did to close the door.

Turning around, still crouched, the Kid surveyed his surroundings. The big guy and the bald guy stared straight at him with wide eyes.

The Kid's abilities allowed him to go unnoticed, usually. But sometimes, the minds of the people that would normally just gloss over his presence just couldn't accept that something wasn't actually there. Times like when a door opens and closes all on its own. That sort of thing made a person's brain look for a reason.

"Is he a ghost?" the big guy whispered to baldy.

"No," the bald man whispered back, disdain in his voice, "I think that's the Kid. The one who attacked the boss in that bar a few weeks ago."

"He's hard to see," the big guy said, "you sure he isn't a ghost? Maybe the Kid died, and instead of being a dead body, he's a ghost."

The bald man considered this.

The Kid took advantage of this hesitation and reached out with his mind to touch the thugs' thoughts.

The dead seek revenge on those who hurt the things they loved. The Kid pushed that thought on the two men. *Jakdin hurt this city, the city the Kid loves.*

It wasn't perfect. The Kid had never tried something like this before, introducing a complex idea to his targets. Usually it was something easy, like he wasn't there, or that a cat is a dog, or that a wagon is on fire. This was much more difficult.

The two men stared at the Kid, considering what to do.

"What the hell are you two yapping about?" Weasel-face said, looking into the room, "I thought we told you to shut it, the boss and I are talking."

"But it's a ghost," the big guy said, pointing at the Kid.

Weasel-face looked in the direction that the thug indicated, squinting as if trying to make something out. His eyes went wide as the Kid slowly became visible to him.

The Kid sighed, stood upright, and threw Edsumar across the room.

The dagger embedded itself into Weasel's throat, and the man stumbled backwards into the room he'd come out of, clutching the weapon in his neck.

The two other men looked from their friend to the Kid.

"Come on, boys," the Kid said, striding towards the door, "we ghosts kill anyone who chuzzes with us. Help me out, and I won't haunt you."

The two men nodded and turned to follow the very real apparition, who strolled past them and into the room beyond. Both saw that the spirit now had its dagger back in its hand, and that the blade was as white as a ghost, too.

"Ghost dagger," baldy whispered, turning to follow the kid, pulling out his own dagger.

"Yeah," the big guy agreed, drawing out a wide buck knife and moving into the room.

Knives flew.

The Kid had already dropped to the floor, rolling to one side and throwing Edsumar at Jakdin. The white weapon missed, sticking into the wood paneling beyond the man standing behind a desk, an array of throwing blades on the wooden surface in front of him. The blades shone wetly.

The big lackey stared down at two blades in his chest, then slipped to his knees, reaching for the knives. He fell forward onto his face, pushing the blades deeper into his torso. One tore through the back of the man's shirt, blood spreading around it.

"Aw," baldy choked back a sob, looking at his fallen friend, "why'd you have to go and do that?"

A dagger appeared in baldy's forehead as Jakdin took advantage of the distraction. The man fell backwards to the ground, empty eyes staring at the ceiling.

"Is that a magical dagger?" Jakdin gestured over his shoulder at the weapon stuck in the wall behind him with a thumb, and turned towards the Kid, who was still prone on the floor. "Too bad I had a protection to guard me from such things. Should also protect me from your damned tricks. But that'll be a nice prize for me to remember you by once you're dead. You know…in about thirty seconds."

Jakdin's hands blurred as he snatched knives from the desk in front of him and threw them at the Kid.

The Kid rolled backwards and to his feet, tearing the poisoned weapon from baldy's forehead as he moved past the dead man.

He couldn't feel Edsumar's thoughts, and the dagger wouldn't return to his hand.

The Kid threw the knife he'd grabbed, and Jakdin leaned to one side, avoiding it, throwing two more at the Kid.

Grabbing the weapons with his mind, the Kid slowed and turned them in a thought, then with a thrust of his hands the two blades shot back at Jakdin.

The thug looked down at the twin blades in his chest, his mouth working as he stumbled into the wall behind him. His hand reached for Edsumar, gripping it and pulling the magical weapon from the wall as he slid down the paneling to the floor.

The Kid's nemesis stared at the weapon in his hand, then slowly turned to look at the Kid with amazement, before gurgling up a bubble of blood.

The light went from the man's eyes as they lost focus and his head dropped to his chest.

Calling to Edsumar, the blade appeared in his hand as his enemy died, his protections gone.

The Kid knew he'd need others to help with the next part.

He moved to the hallway, began banging on doors, shouting that Jakdin was dead, and that everyone needed to defend their homes from this invasion.

People peeked out of doors and listened to his rallying shouts.

I found her. Esperanza's voice whispered on the wind. *Follow my words and come to me. Let us end this.*

Chapter 27

The undead shied away from Esperanza as she strode down the center of the road, a ball of lightning darting off to brighten a dark corner, shooting across the street to illuminate something there, and then zipping around her in an upward spiral to cast a white pool of light around her form.

The priestess moved with purpose and drive, her body language speaking of confidence and poise. Wind whipped around, moving her grey robes, and causing bits of trash to scatter.

The sky overhead responded to the woman's mood and attitude; clouds raced across the firmament above the city, circling inward to a spiral focused directly above her.

A mob of undead, about twenty, lurched into the street from a side alley. They turned slowly, looking for their next quarry. Spotting the lone figure, they staggered into a run and came towards her.

Esperanza never broke stride.

With a wave of her hand, the ball of lightning shot forward and passed directly through the first creature's head, causing it to shatter. As the zombie-like abomination fell to the ground, the electrical sphere repeated the movement another four times on other members of the dead mob.

The remaining fifteen walking dead were within a couple meters of Esperanza, and she raised her arms above her, then jerked them to the ground.

The surrounding winds sharpened and whistled through the wooden porch posts, making business signs wave and creak on their chains. The closest creatures, caught in a half dozen dust devils, lifted into the air, then followed the motion of the woman's hands. Smashing to the ground, their bodies exploded from the impact, and moist bits scattered across the cobblestone road.

The ball of lightning returned to Esperanza's side, and the priestess cupped her hands and blew into them. Her voice started as a whisper and rose to a booming growl, echoing off the stone walls around her.

Throwing her arms wide, then clapping her hands together, she created a thunderous explosion that threw the remaining dead minions backwards. The ones that hit walls stopped moving immediately, the ones that hit wagons or railings tore in half, and still struggled towards her.

"Clean this up," the woman said to her tag-along globe of energy, and the small orb rumbled a bit of thunder of its own, then darted off to obey.

The few monsters still moving were cooked with jagged bolts of lightning as Esperanza turned down the next street, her ball of lightning joining her moments later, dancing a little jig around her.

The priestess called upon the wisdom of Latress, asking for guidance in finding the greatest threat to the city and its people.

The ball of lightning flew around her, stopping for a moment at each cardinal point and pulsing. Zipping to the west, it pulsed purple, and Esperanza turned in that direction.

After traveling another eight blocks, screams made Esperanza turn. A woman and three men backed into an alley, standing in front of and protecting a handful of small children.

Two creatures, human in shape but not in nature, crouched at the mouth of the alley, hissing and lurching forward, preparing to launch themselves at their prey.

Esperanza knew that these kids, if they survived, would never be the same. War changed people and shattered minds in ways others would never fathom.

Calling upon the winds, Esperanza whipped her hand forward like she'd seen a man in the circus do when taming the lion. The air solidified, ten meters away from her, and her wind whip tore into one of the things threatening the people. It turned and hissed at her, then bounded in her direction.

The second leapt at the families in the alley.

Esperanza brought one hand up calmly and clenched her fist. Wagons from each side of the street, caught in the hurricane force gale, flew together and crushed the undead monster in midair.

As the wagons fell to the ground, the priestess's other hand reached forward, and a fist of raging wind plucked the distant foe from the air. The creature was flung upward to a height that the sound of its threatening hiss disappeared, only to come back into range when it plummeted to the ground.

The body hit the cobblestones with a wet thud and stopped moving.

"Go," Esperanza pointed back the way she'd come from, "go with the blessing and protection of Latress. Seek the inn called, The Shooting Breeze, and you'll find safety there. Those of you who can fight, wait for my call, and I'll lead you against these monsters."

The woman turned away from the people without looking to see if they had obeyed, striding towards her pulsing guide as it weaved through the streets towards her goal.

A dark, cloaked form drifted from an alley to block Esperanza's path, its arms held wide, its face hidden in the folds of its fluttering hood.

The being floated a half meter off the ground, cold radiating out from it.

Esperanza's sphere darted forward at her gesture, making a beeline for the thing blocking the way, sparking.

The undead didn't move except to raise its hands, which were incorporeal and glowed with a dim, eerie blue light.

The orb shot at the thing, and faster than Esperanza could follow, the apparition caught her little globe.

Raising its fist, the phantom showed Esperanza the orb in its hand, then squeezed. Electrical sparks rained down on the stones below the specter, and the wind carried away a hollow sound of mocking laughter.

The wraith threw back its cowled face and howled. A banshee scream ripped from the spirit, echoing off the surrounding buildings.

Birds dropped from rooftops and awnings, dead, onto the street. A cluster of rats in the alley to Esperanza's left burst into a violent frenzy, tearing into one another. The glass of the shop closest to the phantom frosted over, cracked, and shattered.

Dozens of distant howls answered the call, screams echoing back to the small street in the dark. There would be more. They were coming, and they'd be here soon.

Esperanza scoffed. She pointed the toe of her right foot at the ground a half meter in front of her and spun in a lazy circle. Moisture gathered at the line she created in the surrounding air.

The priestess narrowed her eyes at the thing floating a meter off the ground in front of her, smiled, then calmly closed her eyes and raised her hands above her—and her voice in prayer to Latress.

The screams and howls of the approaching intangible hunters grew louder, and dogs raised their voices in terror, cats screeched in the night, and horses screamed in their passing.

The spiral of clouds above spun faster, twisting into itself. A funnel descended from the stratus and approached the ground. Mists and fogs roiled from alleys, sewers, and side streets, filling the entire area with thick, humid air.

The phantasm's reinforcements burst into the crossroads, wailing and angry, their sightless eyes turning to face their holy foe. Moisture trailed behind their ethereal forms as they rushed across the square to their enemy.

The twisting clouds from above dropped around the priestess, cocooning her in a furious tornado, creating an impenetrable wall between her and her aggressors.

The specters shot through the wet air, dashing themselves against the wall of weather.

"We may not be able to reach you," breathed the wraith across the road, "but neither can you reach us, or your final goal."

Whispered laughter, that strained sanity, filled the street.

"Wanna bet," Esperanza said, cocking her head and raising one eyebrow, "let's see if I can show you just how wrong you are."

Calling out to her goddess, smiling as she did, the clouds lit up with rolling heat lightning. The bursts of electrical energy followed the conductive moisture, being drawn down from the sky and into the town square. The area lit up, and the undead wraiths within the fog, mists, moisture, and clouds were wreathed and penetrated with the lightning.

The screams from the creatures changed drastically from anger and hunger, to pain and fear.

Within the span of a long breath, the creatures were forever destroyed, and the night fell silent.

The mists parted, and the funnel cloud drew back into the heavens, and the only sound remaining was that of a dog barking in the distance.

Esperanza was on her knees, panting from the exertion. She knew she couldn't show fear to those things; they fed on fear. Only her self-assurance shook their own confidence. That, and a million kilojoules of chuzzing lightning.

Holding a hand out to one side, she called another orb of electricity to her. It popped into existence, then darted away to explore and scout.

After a moment's thought, she called a second one, then a third, and then a fourth ball of lightning. These three circled her in a protective ring that, from a distance, looked a lot like the nuclear power symbol.

The priestess pushed to her feet, leaning over with her hands on her knees to catch her breath and let her head stop spinning.

She focused on the little knife on her belt until her vision cleared.

"That took a little more out of me than I realized," she said to no one in particular, though one ball of energy zipped to her and hovered a half meter in front of her face, as if listening to her. It bobbed when she smiled at it, then darted back to its task of protecting her.

On legs that steadied with each step, the woman moved towards her final target.

Following the pulsing orb for another ten minutes brought the priestess to the aeifain and dasism sanctuary in the northwest quadrant of Durgan's Keep—where the necromancer had taken up residence, claiming it as her personal throne room.

The area was designed and grown using magic, and the beautifully sculpted structures intertwined with trees, bushes, and other natural elements that rose into the air or wove along the ground. Now, the trees were dark and broken, and smelled of rot that burst out from their core. Flowers released fetid stenches that attracted roaches and centipedes instead of butterflies and bees. Topiaries were bent and twisted, knotted into mocking representations of tortures.

Fountains once dotted the parks and gardens here. The pools and basins were now thick with slow-running liquid that resembled the ichor that comes from a running sore. The sprays of water that had once danced above the artistic statuary of the ponds, now dribbled and burbled out of the pipes from below the city, as the putrescence leaked back down into the water supply.

Deer had once prospered within the sanctuary, grazing with safe leisure. Rabbits, squirrels, chipmunks, raccoons, and other animals had scampered through the trees and grass, playing and feeding without threat.

Now, structures built of antlers and bones marked the area, curtained walls and roofs made of hide and fur covering them. The smaller animals scurried frantically through twisting roots and underbrush, attacking one another when they crossed paths.

The entire area was heavy with the fetid miasma of death and rot. It was like the weight of depression and anxiety that Esperanza had battled her whole life had been given form and a home where it could fester and grow.

The darkness inside her pushed up, memories of bottles of pills and alcohol rose to the front of her mind, rearing back and threatening to overwhelm her.

The broken form of the aeifain sanctuary, with decay and deterioration bursting out from under its pretty skin was so similar to what Esperanza had felt for so long, it would be easy to give in to the feelings within her head, heart, and soul.

Or she could fight.

She had the choice; there were two options, and the answer she decided to give wasn't the easy one.

She called to those who'd been trailing a couple of blocks behind her. The few had grown into a small mob.

"Come to me," she said in a raised voice, "we will free Durgan's Keep and destroy these foul monsters!"

She then focused inward, gripping her knife.

I found her. Esperanza's voice whispered on the wind. *Follow my words, and come to me. Let us end this.*

Chapter 28

The three gathered outside of the warped sanctuary. The townspeople they'd gathered surrounded the park, attacking and bringing down any of the undead, human gangs, or anything else that came close.

"Torr, grant me the skill and patience in this battle, guide my blade, and bring the fire and passion to my soul to overcome this challenge," Torrents's hands rested on the pommel on his downward facing sword, his eyes raised towards the sky.

"You're a religious man?" the Kid asked as the barbarian wrapped up his prayer.

"Not really," Torrents shook his head, "but this guy apparently followed a handful of gods. Jonath, Senaria, Chanian, and Torr. Torr's the god of combat, but not battle. It seems there's a very definitive line between the two subjects."

"You know," the Kid tilted his head, "it's really weird watching such a sloped forehead Neanderthal speaking so intelligently. Do you think you could grunt, pick your nose, or scratch yourself once in a while to balance it out?"

"Bite me," Torrents turned away to survey the situation.

"See?" the Kid laughed. "That's more barbarian-like. Now just hunch your shoulders and burp after saying it."

"Are you even paying attention?" Esperanza shot a sour look over her shoulder at the Kid. "Did you hear anything I said?"

"Yeah," the Kid moved up next to the priestess, "this bitch, Aku'ji the Necromancer who is infamously 'Dead and Awake', has taken control, even broken a beautiful park with her evil and her icky minions. The whole place is rigged, and it'll really mess up anyone going in."

"It gets in your head, too," Esperanza said forcefully. "Did you hear that part?"

The Kid nodded, looking across what was now a wasteland, his eyes scanning for anything that might help them or give them a clue what they were facing.

"Gets in your head?" The Kid cocked his head at the priestess. "The place, or Aku'ji gets in your head?"

"I'm not sure," Esperanza looked confused, "I just felt, something, when I went near it."

"Well," the Kid strode towards the wrought-iron gate, "my head is pretty crowded right now, and if she's getting into all three of our heads, she's going to be spread pretty damned thin, and better look out because this is my city, and we don't take kindly to this sort of behavior."

With a shrug, Torrents followed the Kid, lifting his sword to his shoulder.

Esperanza sighed, pulled herself up from her knees, looked at her four crackling orbs of lightning, and then trudged after the other two.

Torrents screamed as the vines, holding him by each limb, pulled outward and stretched him to his limits.

"Some damned overgrown broccoli will NOT draw and quarter me!" the barbarian yelled.

The man tensed his muscles, pulling his hands and feet in closer to him to stop from being ripped apart at the shoulders and hips.

Thin darts shot across the clearing, and thorns dotted the man's neck and chest, the projectiles sinking into his skin. The poison from the plant's spines rushed into the man's veins, and his vision—which was focused on his sword laying below his feet—blurred and swirled.

The barbarian blinked, and the world changed.

He was in a hospital, staring up at the fluorescent lighting above him. Voices spoke to the left of him in hushed tones. They spoke of his accident, and how he wouldn't ever walk again. They were concerned how he'd take it, and how it would change his life now that he couldn't play sports again.

Then a woman's voice asked, too loudly, and it carried clearly to him, if anyone had let him know his father had died in that accident.

The other voices hushed the one who asked, but Torrence's eyes were already blurring as his throat tightened.

The gardens came back into view, a vine now wrapped around the man's thick neck. He'd released his muscles, and was being once more stretched to his limits. The plants pulled, and the world turned into an explosion of color in front of his eyes as the pain burst in his body.

The physical therapist watched his patient as the man held Torrence's knee between both hands.

"You did good," the doctor said, "and from the look on your face, I'd say you felt something there."

The man gently placed Torrence's foot back into the stirrup and stood up.

"Torrence, you've made a lot of progress," the man consulted a tablet on the counter beside him, "and I think you'd be an excellent candidate for that experimental surgery we discussed. With nanotechnology making the advances it is with the help of companies like Jones Industries—and no, they didn't pay me to say that, I just like what they've been doing—you've got a good chance of walking and doing all the things a normal person does."

The doctor looked at Torrence, waiting for a reply.

"You drove here on your own today, right?" The Doctor squatted in front of the wheelchair that Torrence sat in. "First time using the car without someone sitting next to you, right? That's forward movement, Torrence. And you have a girlfriend—okay, you have been talking to a girl, and she knows your situation, and you two even went out, twice—and that could lead to something. You have a lot to live for, a lot to look forward to. You can be the miracle everyone talks about."

Torrence felt the dead weight of his legs, and his arms wouldn't move, and his eyes watered as he struggled for a breath under the pressure of the conversation.

And something else.

"Do you want to go home, Torrence?" the Doctor asked, but it was a woman's voice now; rough, angry, and almost a growl. "Do you want to return to your old life, full of promise and possibility? Or do you want to give up and die?"

Torrence knew this question. He'd asked himself this. The voices in the arena had asked him this same thing. And now, he answered it one last time.

The vines snapped, and the barbarian raised his defiant voice in a battle cry.

The Kid rolled across the ground, small furry creatures clinging to him, biting and gnawing. Any one bite was annoying and a nuisance, but dozens of them at one time caused shooting pain through the Kid's whole body.

It reminded her, *No,* the Kid thought, *I am not her anymore, I am him.*

The sharp pain was everywhere at once as Jen sat up in the wide beige chair; it made that unique sound that only fake leather makes. Her meds sat in a small paper cup on the rolling side tray, beside a Styrofoam cup full of ice chips that were slowly melting.

Screeck, Jen thought, *that's the sound that the chair makes.*

"Are you comfortable, Jen?" the nurse asked. "How're your pain levels today?"

"Yes," Jen lied, "I'm fine, they're fine. We're all fine here today."

She didn't feel like having the pity. She didn't want a new nurse asking her if her family was going to visit soon. They weren't; she didn't have any. And that made the new staff members make that face. It was so similar to the face they made when she said her pain was bad, but it was more honest and disapproving. Not of her, but of people abandoning their own family. But her family was dead, or just gone.

The staff were good people, but they were just…young. Even the Doctor, who was over fifty, was still naïve in many ways.

"You sure you're okay?" a hand touched Jen's shoulder, and she winced.

Looking up into the woman's concerned face, which was ringed by flowing red hair, Jen smiled and reached up to pat the woman's hand.

The nurse's hand was icy, dead cold.

Jen's attention was drawn to outside her door as a resident shuffled past, leaning on a walker. The man turned his head, and his rotting flesh waggled when his sightless eyes met hers.

The two nurses behind the nursing station across from her room, giggled. Jen looked at them and saw their faces were the same.

"We all die, you know," the red-haired nurse standing over her said, the hand on Jen's shoulder gripping tighter, "it's the only way to truly end the pain, Jen. Don't you want the pain to go away, Jen?"

Jen tore her eyes from the dead things doing the mundane tasks at the desk across the hall and looked at Nurse Aku'ji.

The short woman smiled, her eyes intense and wide, her hair writhing like a gentle breeze was passing through it.

"You're allowed to give up, Jen," the necromancer said, her voice almost compassionate. "It's okay for you to let go. It's okay for you to move on now. No one will be upset. And you won't have the pain anymore."

Oh, she's good, Edsumar said in Jen's head, breaking her out of the dream-like hypnotic state she hadn't realized she was in. *I wish I could eat popcorn, this is an impressive performance. So lifelike, so believable. She even had a little bit of spinach in her teeth from her heart-healthy lunch.*

"How are you here?" Jen asked, her mind fighting with two realities, both of which were causing her a lot of pain, and probably would lead to her death very soon.

"I'm here to help you," Aku'ji smiled, and Jen couldn't help but stare at that little piece of spinach in the woman's teeth.

I'm always with you now, Edsumar silently said, *we're connected, usually at the hip when you sheath me. You know, you might want to roll towards that fountain to your left. It might help get rid of these critters all over you.*

Jen leaned left, her ribs catching on the arm of the chair. She tipped over the side, fell to the floor, and began coughing wet coughs, her lungs having that thick feel of mornings and pneumonia.

Nurse Necromancer—that wasn't her name, Jen knew, but the Kid thought it was funny—rushed to her side, trying to pull her upright to clear her lungs.

The Kid looked around, water lilies swirling past his vision. He pushed further down and hit the bottom of the fountain he'd rolled into. The animals were letting go, swimming frantically to the surface. Something shook him. His attention wavered, and the world dimmed.

I've been down here too long, Jen thought from her prone position on the floor, *and if I don't get up soon, I'll die.*

The nurse cradled her, try to move her upright, shouting for help at the same time.

But Jen had gone boneless. Between that and the fleshy softness that came after seventy-seven years of life, the lone nurse couldn't bring the woman upright.

"I think I'll go," Jen was hard to understand for the woman, "but not like you offered. I think I'll just change my life to something more like what I always wanted."

Jen's body went limp, her head slowly lolling to the side, and her eyes staring into an infinite distance.

The Kid burst into the air, breaking the water's surface, gasping and crying.

Welcome back. Kinda like being born again. Edsumar's voice was teasing, but had a tone of ironic wisdom as well. *Isn't it?*

Esperanza had been fighting for her life since before she'd called to the others. The dark feelings of loneliness, tiredness, and the sense that she just didn't have the energy to even move were seeping into her.

She took one step forward.

The orbs around her dimmed, their movements slowing.

This necromancer controlled much more than just the dead. This woman had discovered more than just rituals of reanimation in those lost catacombs once occupied by Rondarius the Foul. This felt like the black magic that broke the will of those who'd become the living dead, and Esperanza had to believe that she could overcome it.

She moved slowly towards the center of the sanctuary. Two of her orbs fizzled and went out.

She'd stood at the gate as her two friends strode boldly past her.

They hadn't understood what they were walking into.

She saw the Kid go down under dozens of rats, raccoons, squirrels, and other animals driven mad by these magics.

She saw the barbarian entangled by the plants, vines and leaves wrapping and covering every centimeter of the man. She saw his form struggle when the vegetation released toxins and barbs into his flesh.

Esperanza picked up one foot, set it down in front of her, then did the same with the other. Another of the protective orbs winked out of existence.

She knew she had to go on.

She knew she had to go on, but not for her friends. She didn't need to continue to help them, though that was something she wanted to do. She didn't fight for the next step, so she could save the city and help countless lives, though that would certainly be one of the results if she did. She didn't press on, even though she just wanted to lie down and quit, because it would end with the necromancer being stopped, punished, and perhaps removed from the world, though that would be an inevitable result if she continued.

Esperanza moved forward, pushed for one more step, fought for every centimeter, struggled to make the next thing happen, because to not do it was to die.

Aku'ji stood on top of a raised stone gazebo, her dark blue robes draped across her form, her scythe in her hand. An ornate wooden throne, writhing with termites and woodworms, was behind her as the necromancer surveyed her conquests.

Dozens of people of all races, dead and alive, prostrated themselves in front of the red-haired woman, though Esperanza wasn't sure if they did it out of reverence, or because their will to stand had been sucked from them.

Aku'ji the Necromancer turned to watch Esperanza walk towards her. The priestess's shoulders slumped and her eyes lidded, each step ending in a stumble.

"Did you come to finish what you started back in your own world, you pathetic thing?" The necromancer sneered at the holy woman. "Did you come to die, giving up against the struggle of life?"

Esperanza's foot hit the first step, and she fell painfully to her knees, the stone edges of the stairs biting into her shins. Her eyes cleared for a moment.

The final protective orb faded.

"I…can't," Esperanza whispered.

"I know, child," Aku'ji crooned, her smile sadistic, "and it's ok to give up, go home, and let it all be over."

"I can't." Esperanza crawled up two steps.

"Then let go," Aku'ji's voice was rising, anger bubbling up, "like your friends, just stop trying and let it happen."

"I just can't do…" Esperanza reached the top step, falling back onto her feet into a kneeling position in front of the necromancer.

The woman smiled down at her; her lips drawn back in a cruel grin. She reached down to grab the priestess's hair in her fist.

Yanking the daughter of another world's head up, the necromancer brandished her magical scythe in her other hand.

"It will be a pleasure to slit your throat," Aku'ji said, "the moment you give up, give in, and beg for the end to come."

"I just can't do," the priestess repeated, her tired voice gaining an edge of steel with each word, "that!"

Esperanza's hand flashed upward, a small blade barely longer than a finger held in her grip, plunging it into Aku'ji's exposed mid-section.

The necromancer's face contorted with pain and confusion. Her hands loosened, and the scythe fell to the ground with a clatter, while her other hand released the priestess's dark hair.

The barbarian's battle cry rose from behind Esperanza, and the gasping sobbing of the Kid came from one side.

Pulling upward with the knife, Esperanza rose to her feet and stepped forward. She grabbed the necromancer's shoulder, stopping the woman from stepping back, and slid the knife left, then right.

Blood gurgled from the red-haired woman's mouth, and Esperanza moved her own hand from the woman's shoulder to the woman's chest, and gave a small shove.

The necromancer stumbled backwards, her knees hitting the rotting throne, and she dropped into the seat.

The vermin that carpeted the massive chair swarmed over Aku'ji, skittering and crawling into the cross shaped cut in the woman's abdomen and into her open mouth. Within seconds, the necromancer was completely engulfed with insects.

Esperanza turned away.

The kneeling things in front of the gazebo were in motion. The dead that once walked collapsed sideways in motionless heaps. The living that had been sapped of their will and energy slowly stood, and dazedly looked around.

Torrents limped towards her, using his sword as support, leaves and vines dragging from his welted limbs. His whole body was red and swollen from his encounter with the plants.

The Kid sloshed towards them, soaked to the bone. Blood seeped from the hundreds of small bite marks all over his body.

"I hope none of those had rabies," the Kid said, reaching the foot of the steps.

"I'm sure you'll be fine," Esperanza smiled, "though we have to use some vile mixture from PepperGarten…that might help."

"Even if it doesn't," Torrents added as he joined them, "it'll be great to see the look on the Kid's face when he drinks it. Always good for a laugh!"

The big man leaned around Esperanza and looked behind her.

"What happened here?" the barbarian asked.

"I killed her with kindness." Esperanza's smile was proud.

"Kindness did that?" the Kid asked, craning his neck to see.

"I named my knife 'Kindness'," Esperanza held up the small bloody blade, "just in case I ever needed it."

Chapter 29

The sun rose on Durgan's Keep. The city didn't wake like it normally did. The sounds and smells were familiar, but only to those that had lived through war and tragedy.

The marketplace didn't have vendors hawking their wares, instead; it had armed patrols hunting the remaining undead. They built huge pyres at the base of the exterior walls, and wagons full of corpses made trips to throw bodies over the side to be burned. This was the way things were done, because you didn't want to risk grandma rising from the dead and eating you while you slept.

The aroma of baking bread and roasting meat intermingled with the smell of rotting flesh. Those not included in a patrol brought whatever food they could to those rebuilding businesses or removing the remaining invaders.

No one traveled alone through the stone streets of Durgan's Keep that day, or for the following months.

Except the Kid.

The Kid threw himself off the rooftop, grabbing the flagpole above the cartographer's shop with his mind, and pulled himself to it. He crouched atop the thin metal rod, looking over his city.

The thieves' guild had invited him to a lieutenant's position within it, as did the assassins' guild, and the city council. The Kid had laughed at each of them, probably not the smartest response, but he made it clear that he had things to do. He had no idea what those things were, but he was going to do them all.

The Kid checked on Jewlnee and her house, making sure that she and her girls had everything they needed. The madam assured him that Captain Jaimin was taking care of all the things that were required; and right now, the Raptor Rex was on its way to Red Wind for much needed supplies.

The Open Door had become more literal in use, as its name implied, and had been set up as a command center.

Esperanza coordinated medical teams, sending them throughout the city to help people. The Kid brought the members of the Grey Ash guild to help the priestess, convincing them that the blessing of the goddess of wisdom and weather would benefit them.

Torrents spent his days leading patrols. They hunted down the creatures that hadn't been destroyed when the necromancer died. Many things more dangerous than shambling husks still roamed the dark alleys and byways of the city, and they'd continue to do so for a while to come.

Mezk the Damned showed up, just long enough to claim credit and reward from the city council, before disappearing again. The Kid guessed the demon pact had called the man to other tasks, but couldn't be sure. He'd have to keep an eye out for that one.

The Kid launched himself off the flagpole and into the air. Bouncing off the awning below him and across the road, the Kid landed in an alley. Walking into the street, he changed his appearance using his mind magics. He appeared as a young girl, a street waif, who gives flowers to people hoping to get a few brass sharps to buy a warm meal with.

What're you doing? Edsumar asked.

We're done with what needed to be done, the Kid silently answered, *so now it's time for me to have a little fun, and also build my brand.*

We have more things that need to be done, the dragon spirit said in the Kid's head.

It'll wait until after winter, the Kid replied offhandedly. *We also need to help out here, and maybe have some fun, before we worry about the rest of the world. After all, this is my city.*

But today, the Kid wouldn't be accepting coins. Today, he'd give flowers to those that needed them. And maybe pick up a few tidbits of gossip and secrets while he did. And if someone insisted he take coins for a flower, well, then the Kid would have extra drinking money tonight.

Epilogue

Spring on the hilltop was great for business at the Traveller's Inn, and Jack Tucker whistled as he cleaned a mug with a cloth.

He looked up as the door opened and three people entered, blinking in the shady interior of the common room.

"Hey guys, I'm Jack," Jack waved, "have a seat anywhere, and I'll be right over to help you."

The first of the trio was a huge man in white furs with a giant sword hung diagonally across his back, tan skin and shoulder length black hair showing his native roots. His broad sloping forehead and flat nose told Jack what northern tribe he was likely from.

A woman who didn't stand out at all followed the barbarian. She was of average height, black hair pulled away from tan skin, but that was where the resemblance to the barbarian ended. She was not of his people. And her bland grey traveling clothes didn't stand out either. But the rounded cloud and stars metal placard that represented the goddess Latress peeking from under that cloak, did.

Jack laughed when he saw through the illusion of the third person. The young man—probably not even all the way through puberty yet—smiled quirkily as he looked around the room, taking it all in with a glance. Jack saw a cunning and calculating look as the guest checked out every exit, corner, and customer in the place.

There were five other patrons in residence at that moment.

Nomed hunched over the draughts board at a table in the center of the room, his trademark leather cloak hung over the back of the chair next to him, and his hand-and-a-half sword leaned against the table beside him. Wanderly stood on his knees in the chair across from the handsome man, studying a handful of playing cards in his small hands that had nothing to do with the game between the two.

Hue Blueaxe, towering over the man beside him, leaned back in a booth. The large man held the handle of his legendary double-bladed axe and its head rested on the floor. The gladiator spun it with one hand, like a top, then stopped it, only to do it again and again.

Grenedal Dragonblood leaned in close to Hue, speaking softly and pointing at the sheaf of papers on the table in front of them. The big guy nodded and smiled, agreeing with whatever his secretive friend said.

The only other person in the place was an older man who was badly in need of a shave. Croaker Norge leaned over his tankard of beer, staring at the wall in front of him. But Jack knew that the man had taken in every detail of the newcomers in the mirror above the bar. Jack also knew that the man had swiped more peanuts and filled his mug while Jack was paying attention to the new arrivals, greeting them when they entered.

"Going home?" Jack asked, walking up to the table the three had chosen.

"What?" Esperanza looked up at their host, surprised at his appearance.

The trio had chosen a table under a window near the front door. They'd dropped their satchels and backpacks on the floor at their boots, boots covered with the evidence of many days of travel.

"I asked," Jack smiled and tossed the white cloth across his shoulder, "if you were traveling home today? You are the three from Durgan's Keep, the ones who came from Earth originally, right?"

The three froze. Then Torrents pushed out from the table, his hand on the pommel of his sword over his shoulder. Esperanza gripped her holy symbol, lips pursed as she inspected their host. The Kid leaned back in his chair and smiled at the man.

Chairs behind Jack scraped along the floor as his regulars half rose and reached for weapons. Jack waved a hand behind him—not even turning—to let them know it was okay.

"How do you know about Earth?" Esperanza asked quietly, twisting her holy focus in her hands.

"I'm from there, too," Jack said, "and you don't have to whisper. The rest of these guys have passing knowledge of it also, to say the least."

"Do you know how we got here?" Torrents settled back into his chair, drawing his hand away from his weapon. "I mean, not us in particular, just any of us? How'd we get from there to here?"

"Yeah," Jack said, "but I want you to remain calm. This next part can be hard to hear, okay?"

The three nodded reluctantly.

"I brought you here." Jack said without a flourish.

"What?" Esperanza leaned forward, squinting at the man.

"Why?" Torrents's head tilted, and his face scrunched in confusion.

"Because" Jack pulled out the fourth chair, flipped it around, and sat in it backwards, his arms crossed on the top rung of the ladder-back, "we need heroes, and you three needed something, too. Isn't that right?"

The man looked back and forth between the three, a gentle and patient smile on his face.

"Yeah," the Kid said, a shit-eating grin on his face, "we sure the hell did, and I think we got more than we bargained for. Not that we were ever offered a bargain. What gave you the right to do that to us?"

"Really?" Jack quirked his head to one side. "You're getting self-righteous and upset about this? After what each of you were about to do and go through? I mean, you all remember where you were when you left, right?"

They fell quiet again.

"Okay," the Kid sighed, "fair point. But how d'you do it?"

"That's a story for another day," Jack smiled, tapping the side of his nose and winking at the Kid, "perhaps we should look to the future, rather than the past, eh?"

"What do you mean?" Torrents asked.

"You have a choice," Jack said.

"Yeah," Torrents grunted, "I've heard that before."

"Do you want to stay," Jack ignored the interruption, "or do you want to go back?"

"Back?" the Kid said.

"We can do that?" Torrents asked.

"Yes," Esperanza said, "I want to go back."

Her companions turned and looked at her in surprise.

She held up a hand to stop questions.

"Look, guys," Esperanza said, "we've seen a lot of things in the past six months since we got here. Lots of things that should be impossible, and we can't explain, but we now accept them.

"Here," she continued, "we found an inn on a hilltop, with no towns around it, and no roads or paths anywhere near it."

"Yeah," Wanderly spoke from over his playing cards, "definitely not a trap, right?"

"Shush, Wanderly," Jack said over his shoulder, "go on, Esperanza."

"See guys," the priestess said, motioning from her friends to Jack, "he knows our names, he knows where we're from, and who knows what else this guy knows. If I accepted all the other things we've seen, then I'll accept this, too.

"And I *do* want to go home," Esperanza sighed, a sound that was a mix of wistfulness and frustration, "let me see if I can put this into words, hold on.

"Even though life's complete crap, people are just shit, and it never gets better, just harder," Esperanza said, waving her hands in front of her, "and it seems life doesn't want you to be happy, it wants you to struggle and fight, to become stronger, to face the next thing that shits on you."

Croaker was nodding along with her words and raised his mug to toast that last part.

"It's our job to spit in life's eye," Esperanza continued, "and say, 'Chuz you, I'll be happy if I want to be, and there's nothing you can throw at me that'll change that. There's nothing I can't beat.'

"And that's why I want to," Esperanza hesitated, "I *need* to go back, to go home. I want to bring that back with me, and I want to spit in life's eye. I can't let it win."

The room was quiet again, except for Wanderly's exaggerated slurping from his mug.

Jack turned and shot him a glare.

"What?" Wanderly whispered too loudly, shrugging his shoulders.

"I get it," the Kid said, "I understand why you need to do this. But it doesn't mean I won't miss you. Can you stay for dinner before you go, and is Jack buying?"

The three friends sat around that table for hours, well into the night. They talked, laughed, and cried, exchanging information they had never thought to trade until that night. Places they lived, currently live, and who they knew were among some of the topics.

Jack served them his regular fare, which was more than passable. The regulars came and went, leaving through one door, and returning later, sometimes through the same door, sometimes through a different one.

When the time came, the three hugged and said kind words, and made promises to one another. Then Jack went to a door on the far wall, opened it, and waved Esperanza through it.

She stepped through.

Turning back to the common room, she looked at her friends and waved one last time.

"Pretty cliché, isn't it?" Esperanza said with a smile, "One last look, and then I'm gone."

Jack followed the woman through the doorway and closed it behind them.

Then she was really gone.

Torrents and the Kid stayed up the whole night, Croaker happily sharing bartender duties with Wanderly, as both knew it meant free drinks for them.

When Jack returned, about two hours later, just as the sun crested the eastern horizon, he had a short beard that wasn't there before, and wore different clothing.

"Sorry," Jack said, kicking the dirt from his boots, "got sidetracked. You guys need a room before going? Get some shuteye?"

"Yeah," Torrents said, bleary-eyed, "sure, thanks."

"I have a question first," the Kid said, watching Jack's reaction carefully.

The host nodded and hung his cloak on a peg next to the door.

"Are there more?" the Kid asked. "Are there more like us? People coming here, and doing what we do?"

"Kid," Jack tapped a finger to the side of his nose, and winked, "there's always more."

End of Portals, Book 1

280

Sneak Peek of

Portals, Book 2, Demons & Daggers

Chapter 1

Nathan tumbled heels over head, falling down the rocky slope, his backpack clanging and clattering, his feet going out from underneath him again and again. His double-headed battle axe was torn from his grip and flew to one side, his cooking pots scattering to the other. His face hit a rock, his nose popping with the impact. It sent him sideways in a tangle of limbs and straps as the world spun around him, like he was inside the world's largest coin-operated washing machine.

A moment before, he'd been staring down the muzzle of a double-barrel shotgun. His ears still rung with the echoed retort as the man holding the weapon pulled the trigger and emptied two rounds into Nathan's midsection.

It'd been a rough day so far.

Less than three hours ago, Nathan had woken up and got out of bed to the blaring digital scream of his outdated alarm clock. His coffee maker had stopped working after brewing a half cup of Joe, and it was only tepid. But that was okay; Nathan got dressed in his white shirt, striped tie, grey suit jacket, and headed out the door. He knew he could just stop at the local Starbucks.

Once he'd arrived there, he had to work his way through protestors demonstrating about someone's rights being tread on. They wouldn't let him into the building, though others were able to push their way through. Nathan smiled and told them that he understood, and it was good that they were standing up for what they believe in.

He made a side trip to a 7-11 to get his coffee instead. The heavy woman behind the counter glared at him when the chip in his debit card wasn't recognized by the machine, and sourly informed him that he couldn't slide a card anymore, it was the chip or nothing.

Nathan offered to pay cash, but didn't have anything but loose change on him, and had to get a smaller coffee so he could afford it. He apologized and thanked the scowling woman, wishing her a nice day, before heading to the door.

A mother and her three kids were coming in as Nathan was going out, and he held the door for them. The mother marched by, her nose in her phone, ignoring his jovial good morning. The kids were jumping and screaming, and the middle one hit Nathan's arm, causing his coffee to slam against his chest. The lid popped off, and the coffee scalded his stomach and soaked into his suit jacket.

As the pain subsided, Nathan realized the woman was now screaming at him about touching her child, and how he could've given her poor baby third-degree burns with that coffee. She was threatening to sue him and ignoring his apologies, and the sour woman behind the counter was yelling at him to shut the damn door.

He left, still holding his crushed coffee cup.

That was the first hour of his day.

The second hour wasn't much different.

Nathan arrived at a little neighborhood jewelry store—which he owned and had opened thirteen years ago—let in his one employee, Austin, greeting the twenty-something-year-old with a smile. The younger man shuffled sullenly behind the counter and checked his phone while Nathan went to the back to get ready to open. He set up the coffee pot to brew, and opened the safe while waiting. Counting down the till, he found that the drawer was $17.38 short from the night before.

When Austin came back to fill his coffee cup, Nathan asked him about the shortage. The younger man held the now full mug in one hand and the glass coffee pot in the other.

The twenty-something swung his greasy bangs out of his eyes with a jerk of his head and glared at his boss, looking the older man up and down through slitted eyes.

Austin took three steps forward, raised the coffee pot up to eye-level, and threw it onto the floor. The pot shattered and Austin began yelling at Nathan about accusing him of stealing, and how that crap wasn't cool.

Nathan tried calming the younger man, apologizing and trying to explain that he was just asking what happened, but never got to finish as Austin yanked off his own clip-on tie, screamed that he was quitting, and stormed out of the back room with his still full coffee cup.

The bell out front jingled, and then the door slammed shut. It was that moment that Nathan realized that the coffee cup in Austin's hand was his, and not the employee's. Now he had no mug, and the coffee pot lay in broken shards in a puddle of coffee. When Austin had thrown it down, it had splashed across Nathan's slacks, staining them to match his shirt and jacket.

Nathan finished setting up to open the shop, cleaned the mess in the back room, changed out of his ruined jacket and shirt, and put on the only other thing he had around; the ugly holiday sweater he had bought to wear to a friend's party three months ago. He'd won an honorable mention with the sweater, just like everyone else. His friend didn't want to hurt anyone's feelings so, at Nathan's suggestion, agreed that a participation prize was a good idea.

But the third hour of Nathan's day was, by far, the worst.

Nathan had been open forty-five minutes when three men burst in. Two wore pantyhose over their heads and faces, and both had a handgun in one hand, and a pillowcase in the other. The third man had a ski mask and a double-barreled shotgun. He seemed to be the leader, and shouted at Nathan to give them all the money in the register and safe.

Nathan apologized, and explained that the money had been deposited the night before, and that he only had the hundred dollars in the register, minus the $17.38 it was short.

The man in the ski mask shouted that he hadn't stole the damned money. That made Nathan pause, look at the robber, then ask, 'Austin?', before turning away at the sound of shattering glass.

The pantyhose guys were breaking glass cases with their guns and snatching different rings, watches, necklaces, and other jewelry from the broken displays.

The back of the cases were open, but the men still chose to break the glass instead of just reaching around the case.

Nathan tried to tell them that they could just reach in the open door behind the counter, but ski mask jabbed the gun into Nathan's gut to get his attention. That's when both barrels went off.

Nathan had looked down, and seen the gaping hole in the sweater he wore—wondering what else he could change into—as the world spun, and went dark.

In the blink of an eye, he was outside in the sun, and falling down a rocky slope.

He slid to a stop, laying on his back and staring up into a crisp, clear sky tinged with green. Blinking, Nathan thought his eyes were playing tricks on him. It was like his vision was blurry, but it made the color weird instead of the picture fuzzy. It reminded him of his grandparent's TV when he was kid, with the corners of the screen losing their color tint and turning a bleary grey.

He worked his jaw, sand grinding between his teeth, and slowly moved each limb to see what condition it was in. To top it all off, his beard was caught in his chainmail shirt, forcing his chin to his chest.

That was when Nathan realized he didn't have a beard, or chainmail, or a battle axe a couple minutes ago. But he had all those things now.

He jerked his hands in front of his face, his shoulders locking in complaint and tangling on the straps of his backpack. His thick fingers were callused, and his hairy knuckles were coated with the orange dirt of this region of the Crescent Desert.

His mind grabbed at the name of the area he was in, wondering how he could know that, and discarding the fact that these weren't the same hands he had a few minutes ago.

A roaring noise blended with a dozen screeches, the former coming from up the hill, and the latter from all around him.

Sitting up, Nathan looked towards the roar.

A creature, a thing was a better way to describe it, stood nearly three-meters tall lurching towards him. It had the head of a vulture, but jointed and segmented legs like an insect. The monstrosity's chest was a thick leathery barrel, creased with chitinous, overlapping scales, each the size of a dinner plate.

The screeching came from smaller creatures, something that looked like petite lap giraffes—from Sokoblovsky Farms in the Direct TV commercials— that had been blended with the undead cat from Stephen King's Pet Sematary.

These things swarmed towards Nathan. He'd never seen them before, but he knew what they were. The big one was a crigth, and the small ones were jedth, and they were all bullies. Nathan didn't like bullies.

Nathan rolled to his feet and stood his full one-hundred-forty-centimeter height. Something in his head niggled that this was wrong also, he should be another forty centimeters taller, and why was he thinking in metric instead of feet and inches?

His new body was already moving as his mind freaked out and questioned everything going on. He had pulled out two hand-axes—these also had double-heads, like his battle-axe—wading into the cat-giraffe things and laying about himself with the weapons.

Each time a swing connected, he kicked the creature away with a thick-booted foot, avoiding the acidic splash of blood that followed.

The huge monster lumbered down the hill, coming closer.

Nathan looked around for his battle-axe. The weapon was six meters away, having been lost in the fall. The creature was between Nathan and his favorite axe, which he had named Marcid, which in Rokairn meant a female blacksmith.

He wondered, on top of all the other swirls of thought, what's a rokairn?

The knowledge was just there, and he knew what it was. It was him, a species of highly organized, skilled, and talented people who favored mountain and cave dwelling, as well as metal and jewel crafting. And they almost always had awesome beards, even the women.

Nathan tucked his shoulders in, and his head down, running towards where Marcid lay without thinking about what he was doing. The monster came towards him on long, lanky legs, listing far to one side and then the other with each step.

Nathan ran between the legs, and then stood up when under the beast, throwing his shoulders back and his arms wide, causing the segmented limbs to fly akimbo and the thing to lose its footing.

By the time the demon spawn had risen to its feet again, Nathan had Marcid in both hands and was chopping into the thing.

The creature fell under the attack, Nathan's steel nerves and stone-like muscles making quick work of it.

This monster didn't have the acid-blood thing, but Nathan still avoided the visceral spray, because it smelled really, really bad, and reminded him of crushed stink bugs.

Some of it got on him anyway, reminding him of the coffee that stained his shirt just a couple hours ago, or the spray of his own blood when the shotgun went off against his belly.

As his body slowed, the deed done, Nathan came back to his own mind. He looked across the sandy field of carnage with a double handful of dead demonic things scattered about.

Movement in the east caught his attention, and distant howls reached his ears. The pack was on the move, and the hyena-headed man-beasts that worked with the demonic invaders would be upon him soon, along with the actual giant hyenas that always followed that sort of war band.

Nathan's stomach lurched, and he bent over and vomited.

Calendar

The basic calendar is a lunar calendar. There are thirteen months in each year. There are twenty-eight days in each month. There is a new moon on the first day of every month. The first day of spring is on the Equinox.

Seasons	**Months**	**Days**	
Spring	Loen	1.	Ginof
	Hapok	2.	Bestuf
	Axara	3.	Midā
		4.	Therin
Summer	Surem	5.	Uthr
	Santara	6.	Dunwith
	Xaco	7.	Lasin
Autumn	Harton		
	Thon		
	Ault		
Winter	Witen		
	Maleo		
	Frear		
Thaw	Milwen		

Glossary

Aborgas: Small hamlet near Red City.

Aeifain: Willowy race of beings with almond eyes, pale skin, and slightly pointed ears. Often more advanced in arts, culture, and magic than the lesser races.

Akar Lake: Body of water near Ruger Whitley Estates.

Ault: Ninth month of the year, and the third month of the autumn season.

Axara: Third month of the year, and the spring season.

Bestuf: Second day of the week.

Bidj: A swear word mean waste or offal.

Chuz: A harsh swear word.

Dangrazio: Subterranean metropolis and trading post.

Dasism: A race who follow the path of elements and nature. Physically, they are slighter than humans, with olive skin, pointed ears, and almond eyes.

Dioneze City: A broken city on the eastern part of the continent run by slavers. Known for its gladiatorial ring.

Dragon Estates: An ancient castle rumored to have a dragon residing in the caverns below it.

Dargaon's Hole: Ancestral home of dragons in the Wandering Hills.

Dunwith: Sixth day of the week.

Durgan's Keep: A city-state in the far east that was founded by a rokairn and his adventuring companions.

Edgewater: Medium port town on the coast of the Sea of Seron.

Everyway: Largest city on the continent of Teurone.

Ez'rainia-fromton: City of the dead located in the Great Desert. Was the city in which Verl'zen-luk had been imprisoned before his rise to godhood.

Fate's Run: Dockside gambling hall in Tarnish. Run by a woman named Fate.

Frear: Twelfth month of the year, and the third month of the winter season.

Ginof: First day of the week.

Glass Valley: A valley made of glass in the slim desert that was formed when a stone dragon fell from the heavens.

Gray Lands: Home of the Aeifain.

Great Desert: A large desert east of the southern Rolling Mountains, which is home to Rogen the Plague and the Great Desert Empire.

Great Desert Empire: A civilization built by Rogen the Plague and his nation slaves, located in the Great Desert.

Hapok: Second month of the year, and of the spring season.

Harton: Seventh month of the year, and the first month of the autumn season.

Highest Spire: A structure that is fifty kilometers at the base and spirals upward. Doors that lead to other places in time and space are spaced every six meters. The height of this tower in unmeasured.

Hope's Hollow: A small village on the on the borders of the Black Wood and the Wandering Hills.

Humbrey: A Kingdom of thirteen houses that embodies nobility and honor.

Icon Hall: Aeifain home on the eastern portion of Teurone.

Jonath: God of justice, protection, strength, and earth. His symbol is a trident and balanced scales.

Kez'et-dual: A demon enslaved by the Troöds.

Khelikian: God of Insects.

Kord: A twisted gold wire that is the standard currency.

Land's End: A demon-ridden peninsula on the south-eastern most portion of the continent.

Lasin: Seventh day of the week.

Ley-lines: Elemental energy currents, invisible to the naked eye, from which wizards can draw energy.

Loen: First month of the year, and of the spring season. It begins on the spring equinox.

Mage, Mind: Practitioner of the art of psychic magics such as body alteration, telekinesis, telepathy, etc.

Maleo: Eleventh month of the year, and the second month of the winter season.

Malvor: Duchy in the Kingdom of Trysteria, south of the Kingdom of Humbrey. Run by Duke Malvornick.

Mida: Third day of the week.

Milwen: The thirteenth month of the year, and the transition month between winter and spring.

Nine Towers of Magic: Abandoned during the Wizard Wars, this secluded and elite university was dedicated to teaching magic. Located east of the Black Wood.

Nomed: A demon-human-aeifain hybrid.

Northwood Community: The largest city in Northwood, founded by humans, dasism, and other races.

Obsidian/Onyx: God of Magic who came to power when the Talisman appeared in the sky.

Obsidian/Onyx Towers: Black towers raised by the God of Magic to distribute magical tools, goods, and weapons.

Ocean Wood: Lands reclaimed by the Dasism from humans under Kala the Black.

Olde Kingdom: A fallen Kingdom in the southern portion of the Everyway Plains.

Oracle Plain: Grasslands north of the Common Wood, east of the Slim Desert, and west of the Rolling Mountains. Home of the mystical order of the Oracle.

Pantageas: City run by mages and wizards in the northern Everyway Plains, just south of the Kingdom of Humbrey.

Paradise Island: An island created by a dead volcano. Now a refuge for pirates and seagoing folk. Run by small governments and individuals, known for its waterfalls.

Parsay Gevies: God of Luck, Chance, and Dreams. Referred to as Parsay by adults, who pray to him for luck, and as Mister Gevies by children, who pray to him for dreams to come true.

Pek: A silver coin, worth one-tenth of a gold kord.

Pemtie: A moron, ignorant, or stupid person, idea, or event.

Phaz, Day of: A day that happens once every four years. Shrouded with myth and superstition.

Promethene: Goddess of Song and Light. Her clergy is almost always women.

Pyridom of Power: A landmark on the east coast of the continent that focuses magical energies.

Red City: Run down city once plagued by lycanthropes and undead. Located on the coast of the

Red Wind: Located in the Red Plains, this city is known for its crime lords and drug trade.

Rock Crag Wastes: a rocky area geographically located west of the Great Desert and east of the southern Rolling Mountains.

Rogen the Plague: Rokairn slave master and lord of The Great Desert Empire.

Rokairn: The Stone Folk. A short, stout race known for their attention to detail, organization, and dedication to fine craftsmanship. Both sexes are known to have beards.

Rolling Mountains: An immense mountain range east of the Oracle Plain, and west of the Northwood.

Rondarius the Foul: Insane Necromancer

Royale Bay: A bay north of the Sea of Seron and east of the Everyway Plains.

Rugber Whitley Estates: A small community known for the mind mages born there.

Rumay Bay: A shanty town on the shores of the Broken Sea that was once a hub of trade before The Downfall.

Runsk: A warlord-controlled city nestled between the Grey Forest and Diaz Wood.

Santara: Fifth month of the year, and the second month of the summer season.

Sea of the Great Plague: A body of water south of the Great Desert.

Sea of Seron: A body of water south of the Everyway Plains.

Seawall City: A fortified city run by spellslingers in a military fashion, located on the east coast of Teurone on the Eastern Ocean.

Sharp: A brass coin, with one one-hundredth of a gold kord.

Shuglak (shug-lak): Horse-sized herd creature with large round ears, a single nose horn on a flat hog-like snout, and two tusks jutting from the bottom jaw of males.

Shulyar City: Dasism name for Silver City.

Silver Castle: One-time home of the god, Jonath, who built it.

Silver City: Also known as Shulyar City, a city built by the god Jonath.

Sinking Swamp: A swamp that hides the Library of time, west of Trysteria and north of the Everyway Plains.

Slim Desert: A thin desert between Everyway Plains and Oracle Plain.

Spellslinger: A generalized term for a wielder of one of the five types of magic; alchemy, mind magic, holy, conjuring, and elemental.

Stadia Isle: A pirate island in the Sea of Seron.

Surem: Fourth month of the year, and the first month of the summer season.

Talisman: A comet that returns on a regular basis, but now is in orbit around the planet.

Tarnish: Run-down desert city on the coast of the Sea of the Great Plague.

Tarra: Goddess of water and healing. Twin of Torr.

Teurone: Continent detailed in this book.

Therin: Fourth day of the week.

Thon: Eighth month of the year, and the second month of the autumn season.

Torgoth: God of Trade and Commerce.

Torr: God of fire and combat. Twin of Tarra.

Transvartius: A wise and benevolent man sometimes known as the Traveller, the Hidden Diplomat, and disciple of the Walking God.

Traveling God, The: God of innate magic, such as mind mages and wizards. Also known as the Walking God.

Trood: A race from another dimension, that are reptilian in features. They have two distinct species, greys and greens. The former deal in summoning magics, and the latter are chameleon like soldiers.

Trysteria: Kingdom in the northern portion of the Everyway Plains.

Uthr: Fifth day of the week.

Velentian Brandy: A strong alcohol drink.

Verl'zen-luk: God of ritual Magic.

Witen: Tenth month of the year, and the first month of the winter season.

Wizard: Practitioner of elemental magics which tap into the energy of ley-lines.

Xaco: Sixth month of the year, and the third month of the summer season.

Special Thanks

To all the supporters on my Twitch.tv channel, TravisTavern over the twelve days it took me to write this novel. These people cheered me on with chat support, threw bits, subscribed, and kept me going in so many other ways as I sat broken but determined to make good use of time that I couldn't use for much else, except building another corner of my world. They did more to make this book become what it is then they'll ever know.

Thank you to; Kavilon, PepperGarten, DropSM, Lunarfox, Devnull44, SpringFanS, Trin_MusicLuvr, AxelBoost, Rwing99, Picklelady, KeltDubh, Tjintur, TheGreenGoblyn, AndreaLeChat, TavernBotCogsley, RichieMuenster, ChaoticDream3, Bodegazilla, King-Xandor, maxzeetv, MelloTodd, Something_Poetic, The WitchsDoor, TalkingTowhee, and LadySkipper.

A very special thank you to the special people who supported me on my Patreon; Bob Lowell, Tripleyew, and Ethan.

About the Author

Travis I. Sivart writes Fantasy, Science Fiction (including Steampunk, Cyberpunk, Dystopian, & Post-Apocalyptic), Speculative Fiction, Social DIY, and more. You can sometimes find him live-streaming the writing and editing of his latest project from his home in Central Virginia, surrounded by too many cats.

You can find Travis on Amazon, Barnes and Noble, Books-A-Million, and other literary retailers.